GUNPOWDER GOLD

H. BEDFORD-JONES

GUNPOWDER GOLD

H. BEDFORD-JONES

ILLUSTRATED BY
PETE KUHLHOFF

ALTUS PRESS • 2018

© 2018 Altus Press • First Edition—2018

PUBLISHING HISTORY

Gunpowder Gold originally appeared in the July–September 1937 issues of *Blue Book* magazine.

THANKS TO

Everard P. Digges LaTouche and Gerd Pircher

TABLE OF CONTENTS

GUNPOWDER GOLD

THE PUBLIC diligence, which in those days was the most rapid if least comfortable means of travel, rattled into the long courtyard of the inn. Grooms ran to change the horses. The passengers tumbled out, most of them hurrying into the tavern for a bit of food and a gulp of wine. It was a summer afternoon of 1778.

One of them, with a rucksack in his hand, stood on the cobblestones looking curiously about. He was a man of thirty or under, with long arms, a lanky form beneath his dark cloak, a face with a jutting thin nose and cleft chin that looked like the prow of a ship. Blue eyes twinkled as he turned to a groom and spoke in French.

"Where is the innkeeper?"

"Master Rudolph? Somewhere upstairs. Ah, monsieur, it's good to hear French spoken in this accursed country!" The groom, a Frenchman, beamed.

"I want to speak with him, and no delay." The traveler handed the man a coin. "The name is Luther Grimm of Philadelphia. I'll want a private room for the night."

"Let me have your sack, monsieur. I'll send for him, and see which rooms are not engaged."

The groom took the rucksack and hurried off. It was none of his business to assign rooms; but the place was in a great bustle, and everyone busy. Also, the coin was gold.

Grimm stood where he was, his dark blue eyes probing around.

This Inn of the Last Virgin—the name had some connection with the thousand martyred virgins of Cologne—lay in the heart of the Rhineland, in the electorate of Treves, well below

Coblenz. In this independent electorate it occupied a strategic position. Two miles away was the enormous castle of Count Otto von Osbrock. All roads crossed here—along the Moselle to Coblenz, north to Cologne, west to Belgium, southwest to Luxemburg, south to Lorraine and France. Yet there was no village here.

The tavern was a famous place, centuries old, as grim and solid and sinister as the Osbrock castle and reputation. All travelers knew the Inn of the Last Virgin. When the peasants mentioned it, they lowered their voices and crossed themselves, with reason. Built on a hillside, the inn was rumored to run into vast underground caverns.

The diligence and its bustle filled only a corner of the immense courtyard. At the far end was a smithy, where clanging iron and flying sparks told of a beast being shod. Hostlers and grooms ran errands.

A clang of hoofs, a hasty scattering, and into the courtyard rode a man on a steaming horse. A man small, slim, with yellow hair, a little yellow mustache, and a simpering air. The inn folk saluted at sight of him. He swung from the saddle, and taking the motionless figure of Grimm to be a groom, hurled the reins at him.

"Here, fellow! See that the horse is well rubbed down—"

GRIMM CAUGHT and flung back the reins, so that they hit the little man across the face. Grimm's hand fell to his sword;

then he turned and moved away. His groom was approaching; he saw an expression of horror in the man's eyes, heard a low warning in French.

"For God's sake have a care, monsieur! It's Count Otto!"

A hand plucked at Grimm's sleeve, and he turned to see the yellow-haired, foppish gentleman, whose cheeks were undeniably touched with rouge.

"Monsieur, you are French? I perceive that I made an error in throwing you my reins. You made a still more unfortunate error, perhaps."

Grimm surveyed him with sardonic air, wide, thin lips parting in a smile.

"Run along, little man, and play with the girls."

"Your name, sir? I am Count Otto von Osbrock."

"It doesn't interest me. I'm Luther Grimm of Philadelphia."

"Hm! I never heard of the place," said Count Otto. "A Frenchman?"

"American. What d'you want of me?"

"An apology."

Grimm laughed. "Go to the devil!"

"You must answer to me for this," said Count Otto quietly. "I see you wear a sword. Will you use it, or shall I have the grooms take their whips to you?"

Grimm eyed the man. He had not missed the slight flash in those pale blue eyes at the sound of his name. He was playing with fire, and knew it. Osbrock had heard of him and knew his name, then. And he knew Osbrock to be one of the most dangerous men in Europe.

"I'll be downstairs in half an hour—if you're still here," he said.

"I shall await you." And Osbrock bowed slightly.

Grimm turned to the groom. "Well? Where's your master? Where's my room?"

"Follow me, Highness," stammered the man. "I have a room for you. Master Rudolph will be there presently."

Grimm followed to the stairs. These mounted from the courtyard, outside the building itself, to an upper floor. And as Grimm mounted, his brain was at work. He had read much in the eyes of Count Otto; if he remained here, he was trapped. This man knew of him, perhaps knew of his mission.

In the corridor above, the groom turned anxiously. That gold-piece was bearing good fruit. Also, he took Grimm to be a Frenchman.

"Monsieur, your pardon. I also am French—not of this accursed place. I must warn you. This gentleman, Count Otto, is not what he looks. He's a terrible person, a famous duelist. For the love of heaven, monsieur, have no trouble with him!"

"Thank you," said Grimm, with a courtesy he had not shown the Count. "Can you tell me anything about a gentleman named the Vicomte de St. Denis, who should have been here to meet me? Is he in the place?"

The man's eyes widened with a touch of horror.

"Yes, yes!" he breathed. "It's as much as my life's worth—I can't tell you now. I'll slip up here in a few minutes—Master Rudolph is coming now." He darted one frightened glance down the corridor, and with an abrupt change of manner flung open the door of a room. "Here, sir. You'll find the room well aired. I'll leave your bag here…. Ah! Master Rudolph is here now."

AS THE groom scurried off, Grimm turned to the approaching figure.

This innkeeper was no obsequious host. He was tall, burly, with an immense yellow beard; a giant, no less, full six feet four. He must have been at work in the smithy, for he wore a huge leather apron that increased his apparent bulk.

"You're the gentleman who sent for me?" he inquired brusquely.

"Yes." And Grimm gave his name. "A gentleman was to meet me here, the Vicomte de St. Denis." He was speaking in German now. Luther Grimm's forefathers had been German; now the family was Pennsylvania Dutch, so-called, but the language was an asset. "Is my friend here?"

Master Rudolph fingered his beard. "I remember him well. He was here four days ago, remained a day, and then went on to Cologne."

Pinpoints of flame glittered in Grimm's deep blue eyes.

"So? He left no message?"

"I know of none. I'll inquire."

"Do so, if you'll be so kind. I'll be down presently."

Master Rudolph departed, after receiving payment for the room.

LUTHER GRIMM stood motionless for a long moment. Four days ago? The man lied. That groom, who was a Frenchman, knew the truth. Something wrong here, frightfully wrong! Osbrock was behind it.

"And I'm a dead man if I don't get out of this trap," thought Grimm. He could hear the rattle and bang of the departing diligence. "Instead of being unknown, coming here like any traveler, I find them waiting for me. Yes, something's gone wrong, and I'm the goat! Now I'll have to act fast, and be tough about it."

He paced up and down the room, until a tap came at the door. The groom slipped in and quickly closed the door. He was breathing hard, frightened, anxious.

"Monsieur, it—it means my life if they discover—"

"I'll say nothing." Grimm shoved a handful of money at him. "Talk, in God's name! St. Denis is my friend. What's happened? Is he dead?"

"Better if he were, monsieur. There was a man here with one eye, an Englishman; he went out riding with M. de St. Denis and came back alone. This was four days ago. The Englishman with one eye went away—"

Luther Grimm checked the eager words with a gesture. One eye!

"Was that Englishman a stocky, heavy-set man? Was his one remaining eye very brilliant, intensely black?"

"The very man, monsieur, to the life!"

"I knew it." Grimm felt a cold chill run up his back. That man was Mortlake, the shrewdest, most unscrupulous, most dreaded British agent in the whole game of secret intrigue. "Go on. St. Denis is dead?"

"No. I heard a soldier talking yesterday. From what was said, a prisoner is being kept in the chapel of the old castle; he is probably being tortured."

Grimm's eyes bit out. "Eh? You think that man is St. Denis? Where's the place?"

"A mile past the present castle, monsieur, on the little hill above the highway. It's all in ruins except the chapel. I know that two of Count Otto's men are living there—"

"Is Count Otto behind this? Did he order your Master Rudolph to lie about it?"

"Certainly. Master Rudolph obeys him. They're cousins. Master Rudolph is of the Osbrock blood, by the left hand. You must be very careful, monsieur."

A slight, terrible smile flashed across Grimm's face, and was gone.

"Perhaps they're the ones to be careful…. Good! Now, do this for me, if you can do it safely: In twenty minutes I'll be downstairs, talking with Count Otto. I may have to leave suddenly. Here's more money. Have a horse saddled and waiting by the watering-trough, near the courtyard entrance. Can you do it?"

"Certainly, monsieur."

The groom departed, with furtive care. Grimm went to the open window and stood looking out on the fading afternoon with unseeing eyes. Now he knew the worst! Instead of all this affair being secret, as he had thought, everything was known. That damned Mortlake, dean of the English secret service, had nipped St. Denis. *Ergo*, Mortlake and Count Otto von Osbrock were together. This was bad. Osbrock was a power in the land, was head of the secret police both here and in Prussia.

Grimm drew from his pocket a thin sheaf of documents. He was tempted to destroy them now…. No. He would need them vitally, he must risk it. He opened one and studied it thoughtfully: A letter to him from the American minister in Paris.

I must urge you to use every endeavor to put this matter through to a conclusion. M. de Vergennes, the French Minister, trusts you implicitly, as do I myself. Although an American, you stand high in the service of French diplomacy. Now you are working for your own country. France is exhausted of money. The Colonies must have funds. If you can succeed in this affair, it means that a good half of this money will go to our account. My dear sir, I need say no

more. I am, sir, your obedient humble servant to command,
Benj. Franklin.

A thin smile twisted Grimm's lips.

"Fighting for my own country, eh? For my own neck, rather," he muttered. "St. Denis was to get hold of the woman, and meet me here. Well, everything's smashed. He's been nipped. I'm in a trap. I have to get myself out—and get him out as well. Hm! Osbrock is a duelist. He takes me to be a gentleman, and expects to kill me. Hm! Thank the Lord, I'm none of your fine gentlemen. I'm out to get results."

If this was war, he meant to fight—in his own way. He had no other choice, if he were to save his neck, not to mention performing his errand. Luther Grimm, a secret agent, had been of the greatest use to France; but now secrecy was gone. Here was life or death.

From his sack he took such personal articles as he could stow about his person. He changed his linen, changed his hose, and abandoned everything that would not go into his pockets. He wondered what had become of this one-eyed English agent Mortlake; but no matter about that. Now he had to save his own neck, and that of St. Denis, at one swift stroke—or go under. Luckily, sunset was at hand, and night would soon fall.

One last glance about the room; then he left it and went to the stairs. A look into the courtyard below showed him the French groom leading a saddled horse to the watering-trough. Good! The man was faithful, was doing his part.

GRIMM PASSED on down the stairs. His quick eye took in each detail—the grooms, the horses, the whole place. No soldiers here. The last rays of the setting sun were gilding the treetops. Already the twilight mists were curling along the valley.

Now it was a gamble with death—a fair gamble. He need scarcely fear pursuit; but he must work fast and pitilessly, both here and at the ruined chapel. Grimm's lips twisted thinly. Boyhood along the Pennsylvania frontier, Indian-fighting, a

"For God's sake, have a care, monsieur! It's Count Otto!"

year with Morgan's rangers—that sort of training was what he needed now, not mastery of the sword.

Yet, during his years in the French service, until he went back to America with Lafayette to take his place at the front, he had learned such mastery of fence as few other men possessed. Now that he was out of the army, serving the same cause here in the Old World again—well, time would show. He might need all his sword-skill yet.

He turned into the main room of the inn. Count Otto was seated before a bottle of wine, alone, thumbing his little yellow mustache. Assuredly, this man looked neither dangerous nor capable of great things; but Luther Grimm was only too well aware with whom he dealt.

He walked up to the table and halted.

"Count Otto," he said in German, "am I to understand that you wish to fight me?"

"Unless you apologize, certainly," said Osbrock, coming to his feet briskly.

"In that case," Grimm rejoined, "you should have a better reason than you have. I'll give you one—"

His hand slid out to the wine-bottle. Swift as he was, he needed all his speed. Osbrock's rapier was half drawn as the bottle smashed over his skull. The man dropped forward; collapsed, senseless.

A startled cry broke out; but already Grimm was outside, darting toward the saddled horse. He caught the reins and swung himself up to the leather, brought down the flat of his hand, and sent the animal leaping out through the entrance gates.

A din of shouts arose behind, and were wiped out on the twilight.

"A man with a killer's reputation needs to watch his eye!" muttered Grimm. "You had your chance, my friend—you weren't quick enough. Now for your soldiers!"

HE KICKED in his heels, put the horse at speed, and headed for the towering castle with the village clustered at its feet, a mile farther on. He was no stranger to this place, or to these German states. Much of his work for France had been done within the German borders, but never before had he encountered Osbrock, the least known and most dreaded man in all Germany.

And now he was staking everything on the one desperate play here. If he found St. Denis, well and good. If not, he might as well turn and ride for France, his mission ruined, his neck in peril.

The castle rose ahead, and he slackened pace upon nearing the village. A massive pile of masonry above, a somber hamlet below in the twilight. Grimm rode at a canter through the outstrung cluster of houses and barns, picked up pace afresh, and peered ahead for what he sought. Another mile, and he found it, darkling in the gloaming:

A tumbled pile of ruins, the ancient Osbrock castle, crowned a small hill to the right of the highway. Grimm struck off along a track that led up the hill toward them. These ruins were complete; nothing remained standing except a tiny building at one side. This must be the chapel, then. The French groom had directed him aright.

N O O N E was in sight as he dismounted. But on approaching the building, from within it came sounds that whitened Grimm's face to the lips, brought a harsh glitter to his searching eyes. Muffled oaths, the thudding of a whip, a raging voice in pain and fury—a voice he recognized. Then the noise ceased, and as he came toward the entrance, two men stepped out and confronted him. Two soldiers from the castle.

"St. Denis! Where are you?" Grimm's voice lifted in a ringing shout.

The soldiers' amazement was instant. One, holding a long whip, uttered a startled cry and lashed out at Grimm. The second caught a pistol from his belt, and the weapon belched smoke and roaring fire. But the bullet went high, and Grimm's rapier drove through the smoke with deadly lunge. Another blow of the whip, a yell of alarm, and Grimm was upon that man, steel licking in across the frantically wailing whip. A cry of terror and pain ended in a cough. The soldier staggered, dropped his whip, pitched forward across the body of the other man.

From within the little building came a choked, muffled cry. Grimm tried the doors. They were fastened by a huge bar of iron. He lifted this clear and dropped it. The doors swung, and he passed into the obscurity beyond.

St. Denis indeed, breaking forth upon him with incredulous joy—a man ragged and unkempt, chains and manacles upon wrist and ankle. One of the dead guards had a key to those chains, however, and presently the Frenchman was at liberty. A tall, lean man, laconic in speech, swift in action; a good second to Luther Grimm.

"You're alone!" he exclaimed, staring around. "Count Otto—"

"No time to stand here talking," cut in Grimm. "I left him

with a broken head at that accursed inn. Speak up, quickly! You were supposed to bring that woman and meet me. Never mind what's happened—where's the woman? If the whole errand's done, then we'd better hit for the frontier. If not—"

St. Denis caught at his arm with a rasping laugh.

"No, no! She's safe enough. That's why this devil has held me here, to make me talk. They even tried a bit of torture; it didn't work. I left the girl safely hidden away, while I came to meet you. She has an old servant looking after her—"

"Where?" snapped Grimm.

"Not twelve miles from here." And St. Denis laughed again. "At the old Fürsten tavern on the river—it's a little hamlet on the Moselle. You have a horse? Good. I can take you there."

"Take cloak and pistols from one of these dead rascals," said

"You should have a better reason," Grimm
rejoined. "I'll give you one—" The bottle
smashed over Osbrock's skull.

Grimm. "Torture, eh? Then I've nothing to regret—except that I didn't hit that devil Osbrock harder! Come on, come on! You're not hurt?"

"No." St. Denis laughed more joyously. "You devilish American—always in a hurry! There's no rush now."

Grimm emitted a grunt. "I'm thinking of General Washington, back home. If he's going to get any more powder, I've got to turn half Germany inside out—and I'll do it. Come on, climb into the saddle!"

They scrambled up together and started for the highway again, where the darkness was already settling into night.

CHAPTER II

AS THEY rode, they talked, by jerks.

"I was sent in haste to meet you," Grimm said. "I don't know the details; this woman is going to put some enormous sum into the hand of France, and part of it goes to our fighting colonies. You and she are to give me full details."

"Yes; you're in charge, because you know Germany like a book," said St. Denis. "I was sent to get the girl. Wait till you see her, comrade; you've a surprise coming! This old servant of hers had got into touch with the French ambassador at Cologne, you see. She was held prisoner there in a convent. Well, I got her out, and we started for the frontier. I was to meet you here. She's got a carriage, and she is comfortable enough—"

"Damn her comfort," said Grimm. "Has she got the money we're after?"

"I understand we must go to Berlin for it," St. Denis replied, and Luther Grimm swore heartily.

"Berlin! At the other end of Germany! What's it all about?"

"Ask her. I know little. She's suspicious of everybody. She refused to go into details until she got assurances from M. de Vergennes himself. I hope you have them?"

*"St. Denis! Where are
you?" Grimm's voice
lifted in a shout.*

"Yes," Grimm said curtly. "How did Mortlake nip you?"

"So you know that much, eh? It was Mortlake, all right; the scoundrel tricked me neatly. We went riding, and rode slap into an ambush. We must complain to the Elector about this."

"Complaints be damned!" Grimm broke in. "Count Otto is more powerful than any of these German princes. He pulls the strings; they dance! Where's Mortlake now?"

"Gone somewhere—to Berlin, I think. Count Otto has visited me every day, trying to make me talk. Twice they've beaten me. Today he said he meant to transfer me to some underground place at that accursed Inn of the Last Virgin. By the way, you might put some life into this horse. I've had a jug of water and a loaf of black bread every day, nothing more. I could use some dinner."

"Berlin!" growled Luther Grimm. "If Mortlake knows all

about this business, he knows more than we do, apparently. If he's hand in glove with Count Otto, we have to fight the most powerful combination in Europe—Prussia and England! I don't like it, any of it!"

"We can always ride back to Paris." And the rasping laugh of St. Denis broke out. He was a bitter man, this Frenchman;

none of your gay blades. He never shared the laughing twinkle that could fill Luther Grimm's dark blue eyes or transform his lean, square-chinned features into debonair, whimsical merriment. St. Denis had spent years in the Bastille, and would never lose the mark of it.

"If the odds are too great, my dear Grimm, ride home! Personally, I hope to remain and settle my little affair with Count Otto. I owe him for that torture."

"You'd best leave him alone," said Grimm. "You're no swordsman; he is."

"Other things can kill," St. Denis retorted.

They rode on in silence now. Grimm never liked anything he did not fully understand; and as yet he did not comprehend very much of this entire affair. Apparently St. Denis did not know much more than he did. But this girl or woman would inform him.

So, when at last the lights of the little town on the river glimmered below them, Grimm was in no very good humor. The Moselle was invisible. There had been no token of pursuit, but his brain was always casting ahead. As they rode, they had passed the corner of Osbrock's lands; if they went from here to Berlin, they must go back that way to reach the highway that led to Coblenz.

And Grimm was only too well aware that, if they did go to Berlin, they must run a race with death. Well, talk of Berlin seemed rather senseless. The French frontier was close. But his mission—gold for gunpowder, the sinews of war for his comrades across the Atlantic!

"You know who this woman is?" he demanded curtly.

"She has told me, yes," St. Denis responded. "She claims to be the Duchess of Courland."

"Bah!" exclaimed Grimm. "There's no such person! Well, let it pass. We'll soon learn now. The first thing is food, wine, clothes for you; then talk to her."

They rode into a little tavern, and as they dismounted, St. Denis uttered a low word of satisfaction. The carriage was still here; therefore the woman was here.

Another ten minutes, and the little inn was bustling. In a private room, Grimm put his razor at the disposal of St. Denis; a bath, a shave, such garments as could be assembled, and the lean Frenchman looked more like himself.

"By the way," said St. Denis, "when Count Otto interviewed me today, he said that he was leaving for Coblenz tonight."

Grimm merely shrugged. A knock came at the door; at his command, it opened and St. Denis uttered a laugh:

"Ah! Comrade, this is Jacques, the faithful servant of his mistress. So you see I've turned up after all, Jacques!"

"Yes, monsieur." The wrinkled old man bowed. "My mistress sent me to tell you that dinner is being served in her rooms, and invites you to join her. We heard that you had arrived—rather, I saw you arrive."

"The devil! You did well to recognize me," said St. Denis. "Very well. We'll be with you in five minutes."

Old Jacques departed. Grimm nodded agreement: They might as well dine with the lady as here; it would save time.

Another five minutes, and they entered another room, softly bright with many candles. A table was set with steaming dishes; old Jacques stood waiting.

"Madame," said St. Denis dryly, "allow me to present M. Luther Grimm."

"Of Philadelphia," added Grimm, as he bowed over the girl's hand. She smiled and gestured toward the table.

"No ceremony, gentlemen! Jacques, pour the wine and serve."

Beauty, vivacity, wit—Grimm divined these things in her, but his brain was busy with old memories, old rumors. The Russian Duchy of Courland had been abolished years ago; the last Duke had been sent to Siberia. He could not remember the details.

She grew upon him: gray eyes that could flicker with queer lovely lights; and music in her voice. Then a change came upon her, as St. Denis talked. He accounted for his delay by an acid mention of a man with one eye having detained him. She leaned forward.

"A man with one eye—no, no! Not the Englishman, the man Mortlake?"

"What do you know about Mortlake?" Grimm demanded.

"Everything," she said. Grimm eyed the girl shrewdly at that simple word.

It was remarkable that she should know Mortlake, the shrewdest of English agents, a man who had been concerned in a thousand intrigues, a grasping, avid, cruel man who stopped at nothing.

"Before we talk," she said, looking from one to the other, "let me ask whether you have brought the promised assurances from M. de Vergennes, the French minister."

GRIMM HAD no desire whatever to do any more talking than necessary; his thoughts, reaching ever ahead, were set upon gaining a safer place than this to talk. But he acknowledged the imperative need of making plans, of getting information.

He produced his sheaf of documents.

"Here,"—and he handed her one,—"is my commission to act on behalf of France, signed by M. de Vergennes and by the

King. And here is a sealed letter to you, which you may find satisfactory."

She glanced at the commission, and surprise shot into her eyes. Then she tore open the sealed letter. Color rose in her face; a warm glow mounted in her cheeks; and with a little joyous, excited laugh, she laid down the paper.

"Satisfactory—indeed!" she exclaimed eagerly. "Now we may relax and talk—"

"Nothing of the sort," said Luther Grimm. He got out his pipe and pouch of tobacco, asked the girl's consent, and gained it. "There are just two questions I want to ask you; then we'll know what we have to do. First, must we go to Berlin?"

"Yes, we must; that is imperative," she replied quickly. "Oh, I know, better than you, how dangerous it is. But I've prepared against that."

"All right." Grimm lit his pipe at a candle and settled back. "Now, we don't know much about this affair. And if we must go to Berlin, I tell you frankly I don't intend to sit around here and get my head into a noose by talking. Second question: How do you come to know this man Mortlake?"

"It was he who sent my father to Siberia—to his death." Her face was unreadable. "He is working with Count Otto to get my money. I saw him ten days ago; I know where he is now. You see, we had fled from Russia. My father was kidnaped and taken back there; he died in Siberia. My brother was killed. Mortlake did all this—he was well paid for it."

"He would be," said Grimm. "Who put you in prison?"

"My sister and Count Otto—she is his wife."

"Mortlake allied with them—hm! No further proof of your identity, of your whole story, is necessary." And Grimm rose. "Will you accept orders from me?"

She looked up at him, smiling.

"Certainly. Take me as a comrade, monsieur; I've been through too many frightful experiences to flinch at taking orders from a man whom I trust."

"Thank you." Grimm's eyes warmed a little. "St. Denis and I leave here in ten minutes. Will you go down, St. Denis, get us an extra horse, have them ready? Here's money." He extended a purse; the Frenchman took it and left.

"You,"—Grimm looked at the girl,—"get off as quickly as you can pack, and leave in your carriage. Drive north to the crossroads at the highway; we'll wait for you there, if all is clear. I plan to get on twenty miles farther to Alken, and there get some sleep and rest. There too we can talk. I know little or nothing of what lies behind all this. You're sure we must go to Berlin if we're to get the money?"

"We must," she said; Grimm nodded.

"All right. At Berlin, we'll have every assistance from the French ambassador there, M. d'Evrecourt. He's a personal friend of Frederick the Great. But until then, at least, we'll be in the utmost peril. At Coblenz, however, I have friends. Now, every road will be watched. Mortlake, and Count Otto, will certainly spare no effort to catch us. They probably know that you must go to Berlin."

"Mortlake has gone there now," she said quietly.

"Good! That leaves only Count Otto to worry about. Well, you have the orders. We may expect you at the crossroads?"

"Jacques drives my carriage," she said. "We leave in twenty minutes."

Luther Grimm bowed over her hand, smiled into her eyes, and took his leave.

CURIOSITY? YES; he was eaten up with it. This girl's loveliness staggered him. Yet, for the moment, he pressed down with iron will everything except the need for action. Safety was paramount to all else; and until they reached Alken, he refused to cloud his brain with anything but the one vital aim. Behind this girl, he could see, lay dangers and perils and torments, more sufferings than he was aware; yet the flame-flicker in her gray eyes was unquenched. A good comrade!

St. Denis had a horse ready for him. They paid the score, mounted, and rode out the way they had so recently come.

"Thank God we don't have to tumble about in a carriage!" exclaimed Grimm. "I've had my fill of a diligence—but may have to take to it again all too soon."

In those days travel was the most severe thing in life, taken at risk of broken pate or limb—rough roads, poorly sprung vehicles, hardship and peril at every turn. Yet this girl, he thought, was accepting it with a laugh.

"She's a good one," St. Denis commented, as though he could read Grimm's mind. "Moon's up—excellent! We can make twenty miles easily."

"If the way's clear," Grimm added. "Alken should be safe enough for us. There, we must separate. We can make Coblenz by tomorrow night, and join up again. After that, we have Satan himself to outwit, if we're to reach Berlin."

The rasping laugh of St. Denis sounded.

In time the highway appeared ahead, and the crossroads; these marked the limit of the Osbrock domain. All was silent and deserted in the moonlight.

T O T H E right, looming high, hung a grisly thing: A gibbet stood there, a gallows great and strong. From this gallows-tree, turning and twisting slowly in the night breeze, a hanged man spun upon a rope, as though still kicking with life. Nor did he seem to have been hanging there long.

The two men waited in silence, and at last the carriage of the girl drew up.

"All well, comrades?" came her inquiring voice.

"All well," said Grimm. "Turn on the Coblenz road, here. At Alken, stop for the rest of the night. We'll ride behind the carriage."

Jacques whipped up his horses, and the carriage rolled away upon the eastern road. St. Denis wheeled his mount, and glanced at Grimm.

*"It was he who sent
my father to Siberia—
to his death."*

"Coming, comrade?"

"In a minute."

Grimm urged his horse to the grisly hanging thing. He rose in the stirrups and put out his hand, touching the dead bound fingers of the man. They were stiff and cold. The body swung, and the face came into the moonlight.

"Sorry, friend," said Luther Grimm softly. "I'll pay this debt, some day."

It was the French groom from the Inn of the Last Virgin. Count Otto had lost no time in getting rid of a traitor.

"Some day," repeated Grimm slowly. "That's a promise, friend. Good night."

And he sent his horse onward.

IT WAS a sunny summer morning. They were in the post tavern at Alken, with Coblenz ahead and the Inn of the Last Virgin gone upon the night like an evil dream. They had gathered in Marie's room. Grimm knew her name now; she was Marie of Courland.

She had brought a number of little sticks to the table.

"Here,"—and she put out three of them,—"are Count Otto, my sister Flora—and myself. Here, off to one side, is France. Here is Frederick of Prussia, opposite." She smiled gayly as she put down another stick.

St. Denis sat silent. Luther Grimm puffed at his pipe and nodded.

"You're telling us your own story?"

"Everything at once; and some of it hurts," she replied. "Flora, for example. She's a year older than I am. She's ambitious—halts at nothing. She's greedy for money, power. She's thoroughly bad."

St. Denis blinked. "You say that, of your own sister? Impossible!"

"Nonsense; it's quite a common thing," said Grimm. "Two brothers or two sisters are frequently direct opposites. Yes, I've heard one or two rumors about this Countess of Osbrock. Go on, Marie; why were you put into a cell?"

"Because of my father's will, which left me all the family money. We'll talk about that later." She put down another stick, at the rear. "Here's Mortlake. He's not an English agent now; he acts for any who will pay. And here,"—with a sharp glance at the American, she laid down another bit of wood,—"is the French secret agent, Luther Grimm, who has kidnaped me and put me out of the way."

Grimm's shaggy brows drew down in surprise.

"Is this a joke? I've had nothing to do with you."

She turned suddenly upon him. "Where have you been, the past few months?"

"In America—went over with Lafayette, and joined the army there. Wounded and disabled—of more use here now. So I'm back on my old job. I just returned, came straight here from Paris—"

"And who knows it? Nobody; least of all Frederick of Prussia!" she broke out vehemently. "He's heard of you, yes. He believes firmly that you've carried me off, that France is after my money, my inheritance, that you're playing this game to get a woman's money."

AT THESE words, a touch of scorn flashed in her voice. She went on quickly, but Grimm did not miss the touch, and it angered him.

"Frederick wants that money himself, and wants it badly. He's going into an alliance with England against France. This means, of course, that France can send no further aid to America, to your people there. You see? England's game is won, yours is lost, France is shattered; and sly old Frederick emerges on top as usual. That's their projected campaign."

"How do you know all this?" he challenged. "You, a woman—"

"From my sister, from Count Otto. They talked freely enough of their schemes, when they were trying to make me turn over my inheritance to them."

"Bah! It's absurd!" he exclaimed fiercely. "The King of Prussia isn't stealing a few thalers from a woman. Why the devil France would be so interested in half your inheritance, I don't know. I'm merely obeying orders."

"A few thalers?" Laughter sprang in her eyes, only to be banished at once. "Then you don't know! But you know Frederick's parsimony, his evil greed. You know France and England are at war. If Frederick allies himself against France, Count Otto shows him that he'll get a substantial subsidy from England; and on top of that, a cool hundred million francs in cash."

"A hundred millions?" Grimm stared at her. "Where from?"

"My inheritance amounts to twice that sum."

Luther Grimm felt for a chair, and lowered himself into it, astounded.

"Why—good Lord! It's a king's ransom! I had no idea—"

"I've offered France half this inheritance for protection and safety," went on the girl. "To get the money, I must go to Berlin. That's your affair. You must handle it, manage all the details."

"Wait a minute, now." Grimm straightened up and laid aside his pipe. "They know all this; it's a gamble for a fortune! They know you've escaped from your cell. They know M. de St. Denis is free, and he's a marked man. So, assuredly, am I. They know we must go to Berlin—the end of the game lies there. Count Otto, we believe, is ahead of us at Coblenz. Mortlake we know is ahead of us at Berlin. Every road, every stop, every town and tavern, between here and Berlin will hold peril. Further, we know we must combat Frederick of Prussia, who has secret police; and Count Otto commands them."

"And don't forget my sister," added Marie seriously. "She's more dangerous than any of the others."

Grimm gestured impatiently. "No. Mortlake and Count Otto are the chief perils. Let's see, now: the archbishop-elector of Treves rules this territory from Coblenz. I've met him—an honest fellow enough. There's a French agent in Coblenz. We must have money; mine's about gone."

"I have some jewels I can sell," Marie spoke up. Grimm shook his head, and a smile came to his lips, a debonair, whimsical smile.

"No; I'll get what we need. We must separate here. St. Denis, you must accompany Marie—no, better still, go by yourself. Change your looks somehow, any way at all. You can do it?"

"Certainly," replied St. Denis carelessly. "When do I leave?"

"Now. You know our agent there?"

"Yes. Hoffman, the banker."

"Leave word with him where you are; I'll get in touch with you. Well, what are you waiting for?"

St. Denis blinked. "You mean—go, this minute?"

"Now."

WITH A swift salute and a rasping laugh, St. Denis swung away and was gone. Grimm turned to the girl, his face harsh again, aflame with energy.

"You're a woman. It's hard to disguise you—"

"Never mind, comrade; I have all that arranged," she said, and laughed lightly. "I need only ten minutes to become a very different person. With the help of Jacques, I can stop a mile outside town and do everything necessary. When shall I leave?"

"At once."

She beckoned Jacques, who had been standing impassively in one corner.

"Pay our bill. Have the horses harnessed and the carriage ready."

THE OLD servant departed. Grimm took up his pipe, frowning. A hundred millions! That meant fifty millions for Dr. Franklin, for the Continental Congress—more, for the men who needed everything that money would buy. He looked up suddenly at the girl.

"This is more of a game than I thought," he said slowly. "I'm going into it heart and soul now; it's no trifling matter. I must know everything—the ambition behind all this. Mortlake's, Count Otto's, yours. They have gold for their aim. But you? What's in your heart, your thought? Are you in love?"

She flushed a little, then chilled. Disdain flashed in her eye; her lip curled in a little grimace of scorn.

"You're so extremely virtuous in your aims!" she said, and the words burned. "It seems to me that you, like everyone else, have one object—seizing the money of a woman. Such high nobility, such lofty purpose, well becomes your harsh incivility."

Beneath that acid lash of tongue and eyes, Luther Grimm exploded. His cold poise was blasted away. His eyes blazing, he flew into hot speech.

"After your money? By God, I am!" And his fist smashed down on the table. "If I could get that amount of money from

*"Sorry,
friend,"
said Luther
Grimm
softly. "I'll
pay this
debt some
day!"*

you, from a dozen women, from Satan himself, I'd steal and beg and rob and murder for it! Why? For myself? For France? For my own country, even? To the devil with all that—no! For what flames in a man's heart and soul, for what burns in his brain, for what drives him mad! For his father, facing the enemy with empty guns! For his brothers, condemned to the hell of a prison-ship and imprisonment because the army had no powder or food! For his mother

and sister, alone in country overrun by enemies of life and honor, by hired mercenaries—"

He choked upon a gasp of vehement breath, while she stared wide-eyed.

"That's what it's for!" he went on. "Gold for gunpowder—money to relieve the sufferings of my people—of my own flesh and blood! Didn't I starve and freeze in those damned trenches, until British bullets blasted me out of 'em? That's why I want your money, any money—not for any damned cause, but for the people I was raised with, my own flesh, my friends, the men and women I've known all my life! That's the reality of it. That's the true reason I'd break into hell to get that amount of money, d'ye understand? And I cover it up with fine words—for Dr. Franklin, for the Congress, for Washington! Plague take the lot! If you want the truth, there it is. For my own people—aye!"

BREATHING HARD, ashamed of his lost self-control, he fell silent. The sudden glory in her face, the glow in her starry eyes, reduced him with abruptness to awkward unease.

"Ah!" she said softly. "There, at last, I've heard a man speak. The flaming heart and the burning brain—yes, I know what those words mean. When my father was dragged off to death, when everything fell to pieces around me, I felt the same. Yes, I can understand, and I apologize to you for my words. Forgive me."

Grimm cleared his throat, found no words. Smiling, she went on:

"Balance against that truth of yours, what the rest of us want! Count Otto? Love of power drives him, intrigue, money. Flora, my sister? Pure deviltry, I think; also greed. Again, beware of her! Myself? I want only peace, safety, obscurity. For this, I'm giving up half of what belongs to me. In love? No."

"All right," said Grimm. "Sorry I lost my temper. Now see here. Once you get to Coblenz, you go to the Fürstenhof tavern on the river, opposite the wharves. Await word from me there. Sure you can make it safely?"

"Of course."

"Then get off at once, and good luck."

With a wave of the hand, he was gone. A somewhat cavalier parting, he reflected; but he had no notion of playing the fine gallant. She was a good comrade, not a painted, pampered beauty. And he was angry with himself for having spoken so violently.

Mortlake, eh? An old enemy, and deadly. Grimm had crossed the trail of this man more than once. He knew that Mortlake hated him with a deadly, virulent hatred. He repaid it with a vivid desire to kill the devil.

Going downstairs, Grimm sought the innkeeper and asked when the diligence for Coblenz was due.

"In just an hour, Highness. It changes horses here."

"Then get me a seat—on top, inside, anywhere!"

He had given some of his money to St. Denis, some to Marie; he had just enough left to pay for his seat, and the tavern bill. He saw St. Denis go spurring out and away, clad in some non-descript garments, acquired God knew where. The carriage of Marie was being harnessed; her luggage was coming down.

Presently she appeared, and Grimm, with some desire to atone for his own lack of politeness, walked with her across the courtyard, handed her into the carriage and pressed his lips to her fingers.

"*Au revoir,* comrade!" and she smiled brightly. "Be careful!"

Jacques brought down his whip, and the carriage rattled away. Luther Grimm went back to his own room; the landlord promised to summon him when the diligence arrived.

Disguise? At this, he was a past master; but so far as the crowded diligence went, it mattered little. They would scarcely seek him among diligence passengers. At Coblenz he must get a false passport; Hoffman, the French agent there, would attend to it. His own disguise could wait till then, also.

"Marie is in the most danger of all," he reflected. "There's a lot I don't understand yet. Why must she go to Berlin to get her inheritance, and how get it? I forgot to ask about all that. Two hundred millions!" He whistled softly. "An incredible sum. No wonder that impoverished France and covetous Frederick would move heaven and earth to get the half of it, not to mention Count Otto and her sister. They, no doubt, mean to grab the whole thing. Well, if I win, France gets a hundred millions—and Doctor Franklin gets half for the Continental Army. By the Eternal, I'll win!"

Puffing at his pipe, he smiled grimly at thought of Mortlake. So Mortlake had told lies about him, eh? And Count Otto had backed up the play, of course!

THIS COUNTESS Flora—Luther Grimm had heard singular rumors about that woman. Young and beautiful as an angel, they said, and heartless as a devil. Strange that she should be Marie's sister. Marie—ah! Now that she was gone, now that the tobacco was comforting his nerves, Grimm began to realize what she was. He had time now to think about her. Those great gray eyes, that laughing dimpled face, that look of tenderness lurking somewhere—why, she was the loveliest thing he had seen in many a day! More, she had character. And brains. She was a comrade worth the having. Grimm chuckled at thought of Count Otto von Osbrock. That gentleman must just now be in a pretty stew, and with a sore head to boot—

A knock came at the door. The diligence! Grimm went to the door and flung it open. On the threshold, dabbing with a lace handkerchief at his lips, nodding with affected amiability, stood Count Otto. And he was not alone.

FOR AN instant, Grimm was thunderstruck. Not by sight of Osbrock, but to see Marie standing there with him—Marie, in a different costume, smiling slightly—

Then he pulled himself together, wakened from his stupefaction. This woman was not Marie, after all; but none the less he found himself staring hard at her. Marie in every feature, yet not Marie!

"Good day, monsieur, good day," Count Otto was saying

affably in French. Under his wide hat, traces of a bandage were visible. "Very lucky that we got here before the diligence came, eh? Or you, like the other birds, would be flown. I understand you have a place reserved. Well, I must disappoint you; it's too bad that the lady has disappointed me, but I'll find her later. May we come in?"

Luther Grimm, somewhat taken aback by this greeting, held open the door.

"The pleasure is unexpected," he said dryly. "Enter, by all means."

Caught? No doubt of it. Through the doorway he had a glimpse of armed riders in the courtyard. The words of Count Otto showed that everything was known.

"My dear Countess Flora," said the simpering Osbrock, "allow me the honor of presenting Monsieur Luther Grimm of—what is that strange place?"

"Of Philadelphia."

"Ah, yes! Some place in America, I believe."

The lady extended her hand quickly, and Grimm bowed above it; for the moment he must play the role assigned him. He could not understand all this. Flora, eh? The face of Marie, even more beautiful if that were possible; yet with a sharpness to the eyes, a baleful glimmer, that Marie lacked. Her voice was sweet, rich-toned, like that of her sister.

"I have heard much of you, M. Grimm," she said. "So you're from America! I've never seen anyone from that strange place. I thought you were a Frenchman."

"Others have made the same mistake." And Grimm laughed. "Will you be seated?"

Dangerous this woman might be, but he had eyes only for the man who concealed wit and power and unscrupulous rascality behind the mask of a simpering fop. As his deep blue eyes hardened, Count Otto read the look and held up a hand in quick protest.

"One moment, if you please! Let me remind you that what's

past, is past—my favorite motto," he intervened before Grimm could speak. "I seek the honor of a conversation with you, not in hot-blooded recrimination, but for a purpose. I have heard much of you, and you interest me."

"Flatterer!" Grimm smiled dangerously. "I always pay my debts."

"As I do mine—unless it is to my interest to forgive my creditors." And the Count touched his bandaged head. He bowed the Countess to a chair, and took another himself, unbidden. His air of cool suavity warned Grimm, who straightway laid aside any manifestation of his own innate animosity.

"Come, shall we be friends—at least for the moment?" went on Count Otto. "You interest me. You're not unknown in the German states. Surely you'd prefer to discuss matters with a friend, rather than with the police?"

Grimm bowed slightly in assent. "Assuredly," he said. "You have, I think, already discussed me with your friend and associate Mortlake, the English agent?"

COUNT OTTO smiled placidly at this thrust, produced a snuffbox, and helped himself delicately to the dust.

"Mortlake does not work for England at all, but for himself. The English, a short-sighted people, have discharged him; they have some odd scruples, those English. However, I don't wish to discuss him, but yourself. Your work is well known to me."

"Again, you flatter me," said Grimm.

"No. I believe you were in the service of France for some years, and were only recently in America?"

Grimm assented. "Yes; I went over with Lafayette and took my place in the army of my own country—for only a short time. A wound disabled me for the time being, and it was thought that I could be of more service here, at my old job. So it has proved. And very lucky for my friend St. Denis, too."

Count Otto swept this aside with a slight gesture. His voice deepened.

"So, I get the picture. You're no Frenchman, but an American, as you call yourself, at present in the service of France. Suppose we put aside all personal feeling, all sentiment, and all pretense likewise. Let us have plain, straight words. Just what do you seek? You've taken part in this affair of Courland, it seems, and I do not quite see why. Even suppose you and France and my sister-in-law should win, which is extremely unlikely, what would you get out of it personally?"

Grimm thought fast, trying to see what lay behind all this, and failing. In the man, he could read an earnestness, a certain sincerity; in the foppish voice, an undertone of steel. It surprised him. He decided instantly on the truth.

"For myself, nothing at all. But it is agreed that from the French share of this money, my country shall receive a loan of fifty millions."

The brows of Count Otto lifted.

"And you undertake a desperate game, you set yourself against all the powers of Europe, so that your country may receive a loan? Pardon me—is that credible?"

"Entirely," rejoined Grimm harshly. "Shall I make it so?"

"If you can. You may be reflecting that I am not talking to hear myself talk, but have some proposition to make you. Correct. At the moment, however, I can see only that you're on a par with Mortlake, the Englishman—both after a girl's money. Well, I'm after it also, because it means power, dominance of Europe, the forging of history! But you?"

GRIMM LEANED forward; he had a desire to convince this rascal.

"You're right; the desire to serve my country is merely a vast abstraction. What did I find over there? The forces of my country dependent on foreign aid. My two brothers on a British prison-ship in New York harbor—why? Because their powder gave out, their food gave out, they were captured. My father is starving and freezing with General Washington. My mother and sister are alone on our farm near Philadelphia, with the

Hessian troops overrunning the entire district. Who can help all of them? I can. The funds of France are exhausted; her credit is exhausted; she can lend us no more money. Well, here's a chance to provide that money! Gunpowder gold! And I'll go through hell to do it."

"Ah!" murmured the Count. "That will not be necessary."

"BUT YOU are splendid—it is magnificent!" broke out the Countess Flora, her eyes shining eagerly, her face alight. "Now you've given your work a new meaning, your actions a real justification! Now all will come out right."

Grimm flashed her a glance of inquiry, but Count Otto intervened.

"Yes, I begin to understand the situation. Hm! And you are the mortal enemy of this man Mortlake?"

"That's putting it a bit strong," said Grimm. "I'd run him down in a minute, if I could; yes. Still, if there's any actual hatred, it's on his side."

"There is plenty; he hates you virulently." Osbrock's voice was smooth and silky. "He wants nothing more than your death. He's dangerous. I dislike to work with such persons. I have not, of course, informed him that you're thinking of going to Berlin. He would be only too glad to welcome you there."

Grimm picked up his dead pipe, knocked it out, pocketed it. What was the man driving at? A moment later came the answer:

"Now, Monsieur Grimm, I offer you fifty million francs of that money, not as a loan but as a gift. For France, for your country, for yourself, for what you like! And with it, the life of this man Mortlake. He annoys me. If I don't have to use him against you, I much prefer to see him dead."

Grimm's eyes blazed out suddenly. Fifty millions—a gift, not a loan?

"You offer this—when you haven't got it?" he said slowly. He did not think of Mortlake at all. That mattered nothing, in the face of this offer.

"Further," pursued Count Otto, "I'll guarantee to send your friend St. Denis back to France unharmed. And after him, also unharmed, the young lady who calls herself Marie of Courland. She'll have sufficient money left to keep her in comfort. But—all on one condition: That you leave here, go to Paris, and stay there. Where you like, but across the frontier of the German states."

Grimm was astounded, uncertain; yet he read certainty in the pale blue eyes of Osbrock.

"You're offering me terms, eh?"

"As a friend. If you refuse, you may leave here in the diligence—and take your chances as to what happens."

A heavy footfall sounded outside the door, denoting a guard there. Luther Grimm was dimly aware of it, but paid no heed. He felt stifled.

Without apologies, he came to his feet, walked over to the window, and swung it open. He had need of the fresh air in on his brain. He was facing a decision of the most frightful kind.

"After your money? By God, I am! I'd rob and
murder for it—for my people, facing the enemy
with empty guns; an army with no powder!
That's what it's for—gunpowder gold!"

These two had come here to get rid of him at any cost. They were ready to buy him off. When he told Osbrock his own driving motive, he had given the man the key; here was the result: fifty millions, a free gift—for the old man in the army, the brothers aboard a prison-ship, the folks back home; for all who stood behind these symbols in his own life, the struggling army, the Congress, the banded colonies, the cause.

Fifty millions as a gift to take Franklin! That was worth selling himself, his soul, his honor, to get. For the struggling man in Paris, for the struggling country; but more, for the starving, desperate people, his own people, his own family, whose fate hung upon it. A gift of fifty millions! Gunpowder gold!

At what price? Giving up this girl Marie, and not to any danger, either. All they wanted was her money. They would leave her enough to secure her from want. Probably Frederick of Prussia would get a hundred million. Count Otto would take half as much, and hand over the balance to—whom? Grimm's hand clenched.

Not to him, no. Not a cent of it to him; it would go direct to Franklin, or even to the Congress. It meant that he would betray the trust France had put in him. If he played an honorable game, facing desperate odds, risking the loss of everything—well, Berlin was far away. France mattered nothing to him. Peace or war mattered nothing to him. Let the Old World fight itself blind! He had to think of his father with Washington, his brothers starving, his army fighting for life along the Jersey marshes.

Honor be damned! The temptation gripped him hard. After all, the highest honor might lie in sacrificing all else, honor itself, for this cause of his.

Suddenly he found her face close beside him; a light quick step, a scent of perfume. The Countess was there, appealing to him; her hand touched his arm with slight, significant pressure.

A lovely woman, this Flora, her eyes burning into him, her voice low, a mere whispered breath, for his ear alone:

"Careful!" she was saying under her breath. "Don't refuse. It would be suicide. He has pistols under his coat, armed men outside; he means to kill you. Agree. I'm your friend. Come with us to Coblenz. Many things can happen there. I want to see you again. He'll be gone. Later you can go to Paris, the cash in your pocket."

Sharp incredulity wrenched at Luther Grimm; it was impossible to mistake the implication of her words, her eyes. Clever, was she? Devil a bit. Nothing clever about this sly puss.

The temptation hit him like a counter-antidote; but for her low words, he might have wavered further. That thought about honor, about the honor of dishonor, about selling himself for the sake of Franklin, was sent reeling out of his brain. He stared out of the window.

This was the ground floor of the inn. Beyond his window were the stables. Just outside here were two men, booted and armed, idly talking as they held their horses. Two of Count Otto's riders.

Swiftly, Grimm swung back to himself. Play the game, Luther Grimm of Philadelphia! That old man with the white hair would countenance no such dishonor, even for the sake of Washington's army. His own word had been passed; that girl Marie depended on him. Win the game despite all odds. No forked trails, as the Indians put it.

Grimm turned. He had no weapon; his sword was hanging against the door, and he could not reach it. He knew the seeming fop was sharply, keenly alert. Play the same trick again? A shrewd man never looked to see a trick tried twice. On the table stood a long, heavy pewter candlestick…. No, that was out of his reach, too.

GRIMM CAME to the table and halted, hesitant, frowning a little.

"How do I know you're to be trusted, after the way I tricked you back there at the Last Virgin?" he asked slowly. "How do I know you'll keep your word now?"

"It's to my interest to do so. My actions are dictated solely by policy," said Count Otto complacently. "The more dangerous an opponent is, the better friend he may be. Six months from now, who knows? We may be working together. What's past, is past. I cherish no enmities."

A curious philosophy, thought Grimm; a most rascally philosophy. Apparently the man was sincere. He was watching Grimm with catlike eyes. One hand held the scented lace handkerchief; the other was out of sight. Pistol ready, no doubt. But such a man watched for weapons, not for fists.

"Aye, that's the usual conception of such intrigue as this, I find," Grimm said in a thoughtful voice. "Here in Europe, all you chess-players are alike; you have a smooth, sly trickery at your fingers' ends. Undoubtedly your proposal tempts me, Osbrock. But we don't work that way in America."

"Indeed? I wasn't aware your savage wilderness had developed a diplomatic technique!" Count Otto smiled as he sniffed at his handkerchief. "Just how, if I may inquire, do you work in America?"

"Like this!" And Grimm's fist swung.

The blow lashed home below the ear.

Not waiting to see its effect, Grimm turned and started for the open window. As he did so, he caught up the pewter candlestick from the table. There was a sharp cry, a flash of steel. The woman Flora came rushing at him, poniard in hand.

Strike a woman? Grimm hesitated, feinted a blow, and as she checked herself, he gave her a push and tripped her neatly, sending her in a headlong sprawl. He leaped at the window and was out, still gripping the candlestick. Her voice rose shrilly.

The two soldiers outside had taken the alarm. They turned, staring at Grimm as he came. It was touch and go now. If they used their weapons, they had him. A scream burst from the room behind, a scream so instinct with rage, with wild feline fury, that it sent a shiver through him.

"Quick!" he cried at the two men. "She's killing Count Otto—help him!"

A startled oath, and they abandoned their horses, plunging with a run for the window. Grimm fairly hurled himself at the horses. He gained them, was in the saddle of one with a wild leap, caught the reins, seated himself, and sent the animal jumping forward.

On now to the corner of the inn and around, reining down the frightened animal with savage hand. Here was a street of the town; he swung into it—and slap into two more of Count Otto's riders. They must have known him by sight or description, for a shout broke from them, and their swords flashed up.

The heavy candlestick swung, and like a thunderbolt knocked one man out of his saddle. The other lunged in frantically, his horse rearing. Grimm warded the blade with his left arm and swung around with his right; the soldier screamed as he went down under that crushing blow.

Kicking his horse into renewed motion, Luther Grimm went plunging down the street for the Coblenz road.

Cries rang out; people scattered to right and left. A market cart was upset in wild confusion. Figures were flooding into the street behind, and a wild tumult was in the air, yells and shouts ringing up. Two country wagons ahead—Grimm went smash at the horses, crowded the animals together, slipped through as the two carts crashed.

W I T H A laugh, he dropped the bent candlestick and lashed his horse into a gallop. The narrow street was well blocked against pursuit. Three minutes later, he was out of the town, speeding away at fast and furious breakneck course. Out of the trap and away!

CHAPTER III

LUTHER GRIMM pushed his horse like a madman; mile after mile dropped behind. Inquiring in a village, he found that the next post-house lay in a town seven miles ahead. He pressed on again, the good horse in a lather of foam, ran out the last few miles, and came into a place of some size. He knew that he was well ahead of the eastbound diligence. He lost no time selling his horse to a dealer who asked no questions, and in losing his identity....

It was long past noon when the diligence came clattering in to the post tavern. Hostlers sprang to work. The post-horses were out of harness, into stalls, and the fresh horses being led into place. On the waiting-bench for the diligence sat a man eating bread and cheese, with a stoup of wine from the tavern. Summoned to take his place in the vehicle, he showed himself round-shouldered, stooped, anything but clean; he was clad in shabby garments, a battered old hat, and *sabots* that were chipped and dirty.

Crowded into the diligence with the other passengers, he heard the boot closed, the driver and postilions scramble to their positions, the whistle blow for departure. But no departure; instead came a rush of men and horses through the town, some riders turning into the inn yard, others clattering on past. Peremptory voices issued commands, orders. Two men inspected the passengers in the diligence, then turned to the inn.

The pursuit, the search, had caught up, and now it had passed ahead. The diligence was free to leave. The whip cracked, the post-horn's mellow note floated out; the horses swept into instant speed on the road for Coblenz.

There was little talking. The American sat hunched and braced against road shocks, like the other passengers; his face wore a vacant look; when a commercial traveler opposite cursed the clumsy wooden *sabots,* Grimm cringed a little and made

"Your pardon!"
Grimm bowed. "I
have made an error!"
"More than you
know," said a voice.
"Who are you?"

no response. When some one grunted a question at him, he merely looked blank. These stout Germans had no use for a fool.

Neither did the pursuers, who did not seek a fool at all.

The miles tripped rapidly behind, as the vehicle clattered and thundered on to the great city. Even faster than the diligence, however, was a light carriage which could also command relays of fresh horses at frequent intervals. If Grimm had needed any proof of the qualities of Count Otto and his Countess, it came to him when he alighted from the diligence in the courtyard of the Coblenz terminal.

He saw them sitting there in the elegant carriage, its horses a-steam, watching the passengers leave the diligence. Evidently Count Otto was taking nothing for granted; and for once there was nothing of the simpering fop in his appearance. Despite hurts, despite hard and fast travel, the man looked fresh and savagely alert.

As for the woman who sat beside him, her strange beauty impressed itself upon Luther Grimm at this moment with singular force. It was a calm, almost an ethereal beauty, far

removed from any passion or emotion; he recognized it for the mask it was. In repose the mouth had a slight downward twist which marked a subtle difference from that of Marie; this was almost the only detail in which the two women were outwardly at variance.

THANKFUL FOR the sweat-smeared dust on his face and hair hanging about his eyes, Grimm was half across the courtyard when a sudden commotion arose. To his dismay, two grooms ran after and caught hold of him. A woman, who with her whining baby had sat next him in the vehicle, came screeching, while a crowd gathered instantly. The woman flung herself on the dumfounded Grimm, clawed at him, and from the sagging pocket of his ragged coat triumphantly produced the baby's nursing bottle. She had put it there, out of her own way, as they rode.

A roar of laughter went up. Grimm, vacuous of eye and stooped of shoulders, peered about as he was released. He was, in reality, badly shaken by the incident. A postilion clapped him heavily on the back, with more laughter.

"So you'd steal the milk of an innocent babe, eh? You must be a Pomeranian, you rascal! They'd steal anything. Here! What's dragging down that other pocket of yours?"

Vacantly, Grimm displayed the contents—the remains of his bread and cheese, and a raw turnip. The laughter was redoubled, and under cover of it he shambled away, his *sabots* clumping the stones. A moment later he was safely out of the inn yard and mingling with the afternoon throngs in the city streets.

COBLENZ, QUEEN of the Rhine! Here, without curious questions from merchants, he changed his appearance as he desired. In his present shape he could not very well go to any tavern.

Turning in at a shop, he laid out some of his money with all the naïve delight of a countryman come to town. The sale of the horse had provided as much money as he now needed. With the clothes he sought, he next went to a barber near by and had his head clipped. Here, also, he was able to buy a passable wig. And as wigs were out of fashion, this served his disguise all the better.

Behold, then, an untidy, black-clad, stoop-shouldered notary betaking himself toward the river front and gaping away at the wharves, the swift-rushing Rhine, the boats and the long bridge. A notary with portfolio under arm, with spectacles perched on his thin hawk-beak, with soiled linen at throat and cuffs, and leaning heavily on his stick as he walked, with a distinct limp. Even the smear of brownish snuff about his nostrils and on his linen was perfectly applied.

At length he came to the Fürstenhof tavern, an old and comfortable establishment serving the river trade. And as he limped in and was about to apply for a private room, he once more had evidence of Count Otto's comprehensive activities: Two cold-eyed men, agents of police, were minutely questioning the innkeeper regarding his arrivals of the afternoon. But they gave Grimm a careless glance and went on with their task.

They had excellent descriptions of Luther Grimm—as he had been—and also of St. Denis and Marie of Courland.

As Grimm was interested to note, they drew quite blank here. No lady whatever had come to the Fürstenhof this day. Nobody had arrived, in fact, except a young gentleman from Berlin who was out seeing the world, with an old family retainer to wait on him—and very little money in his pocket, to judge by his pinchpenny manner.

"All these Prussians are alike," grumbled the innkeeper. "This fellow acts like a lord and spends like a lackey! So stingy, just like his royal master, that he had to have the cheapest lodgings in the house."

The police merely sniffed at this information, and departed to make the round of the other taverns.

Luther Grimm secured a room, deposited his few effects in it, and after a cup of wine in the tap-room, sauntered forth. It was the sunset hour, the one best suited to his present intent. Later in the evening spies might be anywhere, would be everywhere. The banker Hoffman was probably known to be a French agent, and would be under watch.

Circling through the town, Grimm found the house he sought in the Schloss Strasse. It was the combined office and residence of Herr Hoffman; clerks were putting up shutters for the night, and the courtyard gates were being closed. Grimm spoke with one of the clerks.

"Your master is here? I must have a word with him at once."

"You're an important personage, eh?" sneered the clerk. "Thus to disturb him when the office is shut for the day!"

"Tell him, if you please, that his cousin is here."

"Oh! That's different. Will you come into the courtyard?"

Grimm would, and did. The clerk departed, to return again, obsequious and most deferential. A moment later Grimm found himself in the presence of the banker, who gave him a blankly puzzled stare and addressed him in French.

"Well, monsieur? You made use of a certain phrase known

to me, but I do not know you—ah!" An exclamation broke from him as Grimm straightened up, removed the curled wig, and flashed him a smile. "Why, M. Grimm—God bless me, I'd never have known you!"

"Thanks." And Grimm chuckled. "I need both money and information. And help."

"You have only to ask, monsieur."

"Have you received any word from my friend the Vicomte de St. Denis?"

"None. I know him, however."

"He should be here. He may get in touch with you tonight or in the morning. Now, I'm using the name of Jan Stern; but I need a passport in that name, also a thousand francs. Can you help me out?"

"Of course," replied the banker promptly. As contact man for many a French secret agent, he was used to emergencies. "The money instantly, the papers by noon tomorrow. I'm wholly at your service."

"Thank you. I shall be at the Fürstenhof, under the name of Jan Stern, until tomorrow night. Could you procure me a private audience with the Elector tomorrow?"

The banker fell into troubled thought; then his face cleared. "As yourself, or as Jan Stern?"

"Oh, the latter! I have a message for him." Grimm smiled. "I have just arrived from Berlin, where the King of Prussia confided to me a verbal and private message for him. Thus, at least, you may inform him."

Hoffman darted him a sharp glance, and nodded. With the eccentric Frederick of Prussia, who paid no regard to conventions, anything was possible.

"I'm to see the Elector in the morning at ten. I can take you with me; yes, I'll arrange it. So you've just come from Berlin?"

"That's the story." Grimm shrugged. "I'm headed for Paris. Inquiries will most certainly reach you, and it'll do no harm if you talk freely."

Hoffman nodded again. "I understand. His Highness is building a new castle, and is temporarily living at the old palace on the Schloss Platz. I can pick you up at the Fürstenhof about nine-thirty in the morning."

"Thank you; it'll be most kind."

His pockets heavy with cash, Grimm made his way back to the tavern.

France was well served in Coblenz!

He had thought deeply about this audience with the Elector, and had determined upon it. He was risking nothing by giving a false message; and it was imperative that he get in a crack at Count Otto. Luther Grimm acted on the principle that the quicker the enemy was shaken and given a body blow, the better. "Never neglect an opportunity; if there is none, make one," old Benjamin Franklin had once advised him.

He made inquiries at the tavern. The young gentleman who had that afternoon arrived with his lackey bore a long and involved Prussian title. Grimm sent a servant to ask that the notary Jan Stern be received. The servant came back and beckoned him.

GRIMM FOLLOWED to a small bare room, evidently one of the cheapest to be had in the place. Before the flickering candle glow, he bowed and stared hard. For a moment his heart misgave him; the consequences of a mistake gripped sharply at him. No sign in this young gallant of the Maric he knew! Black hair and brows instead of rippling gold. The attire of a dandy, the finest of linen, a Spanish cloak about the young man's shoulders—no, no!

"Your pardon," Grimm bowed over his stick. Ever perfect in his part, his very voice had become dry and precise. "Your Excellency will excuse me. I have made an error."

"You have," said a voice behind him.

Grimm turned, to see a figure standing there with pistol leveled.

"More of an error than you know, perhaps," went on the

voice. "And you'll answer for it. Who are you? What brought you here? Out with the truth!"

This was the young gentleman's lackey. Suddenly Grimm's heart leaped. He recognized those wrinkled, withered features. Old Jacques!

"Speak up!" The pistol came to cock, with a sharp click.

Grimm straightened. A shower of gold was disgorged from his pocket over the table. He plucked away the wig, and his ringing laugh burst upon the room.

"Congratulations, Marie!" he exclaimed. "Upon my word, you fooled me completely!"

"You—*you!*" She sprang forward, caught his hand, and stared at him. "Oh, comrade! And I never recognized you, never knew you! Why, I saw you downstairs an hour ago; you were just going out. I thought what a queer fellow you looked! Jacques, it's he!"

"So I see," observed the old retainer with dry chagrin. "And I came near to shooting him, I can tell you!"

During the next few moments there was rapid talk, explanation, surmise. Grimm nodded, to her smiling inquiry.

"Admirable! With the cloak, you'd pass anywhere; it hides what's left of your figure. And blackening your hair was a master-stroke. I trust the stain isn't permanent?"

"I can wash it out any time," said the girl, laughing.

"Good. So you got here about broke, eh? … Well, we've no more money troubles for the present. No word from St. Denis yet. There's the devil of a search on foot. Police were here, are seeking everywhere. Hm!" His gaze narrowed. "Do you know, you're far better looking than your sister?"

"Flora?" A startled expression leaped into the girl's face. "My sister? You've not seen her?"

HE NODDED, and sketched the day's happenings briefly.

"You and your sister are almost twins—or were, before the present change in you," he went on. "At sight of her, I thought it was you; a bad moment, let me tell you! Now let me get straightened out! Does Mortlake know her? He must, if he's known your family."

"By sight, no doubt," said the girl, frowning. "But I doubt if he knows her more than that—probably he's never spoken with her. She and Otto were the ones who had me locked up, and have conducted all attempted negotiations with me. Flora has told about the man, of course. I've seen him several times, but have never spoken with him."

"I see." Luther Grimm got out his pipe and stuffed it, then laid it aside until their meal should be served and over. "Then Mortlake has had most of his dealings with Count Otto, who doesn't like him any too well, eh?"

"Probably distrusts him," she said. "You see, Mortlake betrayed my father, sold him to Russia."

"I get the picture. Now about yourself: Do you lay claim to the Duchy of Courland?"

"Mercy, no!" She broke into a wry laugh. "Catherine of Russia has set up a new duke. I don't care anything about the title. For many years, a part of the revenues were set aside by my father; they were put into the hands of bankers in Prussia, and in the end they amounted to a vast sum.

"Well, when our estates were confiscated, when everything went smash, this money remained in safety. It's now held in trust for me by those bankers. They'll surrender it only to me in person, when I appear and establish my identity. Of course, they know me; this clause is really a formality, but it was to provide against any trickery by Flora. My father was afraid of her, you see. Well, I have the essential documents; and I must appear before those two bankers in Berlin—Arnheim and Pfalzer. They're honest men, but—"

"BUT?" PROMPTED Luther Grimm, as she paused.

"But Frederick of Prussia wants that money. And naturally, they're more or less under his thumb."

Luther Grimm whistled softly. "I begin to appreciate your difficulties—and my own! Count Otto and your sister—"

"Meant to strip me. By turning over the whole inheritance, I was to receive my freedom and a life annuity. Well, I'm free! And I'm not going to give King Frederick one solitary copper!"

Luther Grimm nodded. He could now comprehend that this girl would find no safety or protection in Berlin. Once there, she would be as among ravening wolves. The King would not hesitate for a moment to extort half her patrimony from her. And as for letting her give half of it to France—

"Why," he asked slowly, "couldn't you turn over the whole thing to France for collection? Then you'd not have to go to Berlin at all."

"The bankers wouldn't pay it; the sum is in trust, you know, and I must appear in person. Count Otto was going to bring both the bankers to Cologne—the King would make them come, of course—and interview me there."

"It's Berlin for all of us, then." And Grimm nodded. "And after dinner we must separate, for safety's sake. I'm done up and need a good night's sleep. As soon as I meet St. Denis tomorrow, we'll be on our way. You have money; your disguise is admirable, and you needn't worry. Once in Berlin, go to the Hôtel de Paris. It's a quiet little rooming-house kept by a French widow; you can trust her—she knows me. Wait there for word from me."

"Understood, comrade." Marie regarded him gravely. "Do you know, at first I thought you were terribly harsh and cold; now I know you better, I don't think so. Are all Americans like that? Perhaps because they see so much of those frightful redskin savages we've heard about. I thought all Americans wore rings in their ears."

Grimm broke into a laugh. "No, not all; at least, I don't. But I may take a scalp or two before we reach Berlin."

She smiled. "Well, make yourself comfortable; Jacques will

serve the dinner here as soon as it's ready. I'll step into the other room and brush up a bit."

Luther Grimm sat alone over his pipe. He thought of Marie. He thought of that other woman at Alken, her beauty, her effort to beguile him. A spark of alarm grew in his brain, but not because of her. Marie's words had suggested something to him:

He recalled how Count Otto had been sitting in his carriage here in Coblenz, watching the diligence arrive. Count Otto, giving no sign of the crushing blow that had struck him down. Count Otto, the master of intrigue, hat pulled over hurt head and yellow curls, driving like mad past the vineyards of the Moselle to reach Coblenz!

Redskin savages, yes. Oddly enough, there was something in this antagonist of his to remind Grimm of a lurking Iroquois, deadly and merciless.

<h2 style="text-align:center">CHAPTER IV</h2>

COBLENZ, WHENCE the Elector and Archbishop of Treves ruled all his rich domain, was plump with prosperity and peace, like its lord.

A placid, kindly, middling-handsome man was Clemens the Elector, devoted to the arts, loving justice, a great builder and beautifier of his capital city. Just such a man as Otto of Osbrock loved to deal with.

The ancient Schloss, overlooking the city and the confluence of Rhine and Moselle, was being torn down and rebuilt. The hilly streets were teeming with wagons; workmen by hundreds were bustling about; building materials were pouring in by road and by river. Across the Rhine towered the mighty hill and fortress of Ehrenbreitstein, defending Coblenz against all attack from the east.

Elector Clemens, who was by preference less an archbishop than a ruler, sat in the cool library of the old palace on the Schloss Platz. His episcopal ring, his purple *soutane*, his firmly pleasant and ruddy features, contrasted sharply with the dictation he gave his secretaries. His language could be most unclerical. On the surface he was an absolute ruler, a despot, although a kindly one. So, at least, he was pleased to consider himself.

UPON THE room hung an atmosphere of rich elegance which was symbolic of the man and his position and his day. The morning sunlight was excluded by draperies of cloth of gold. In one corner, on its pedestal of ebony, stood the glorious marble Venus supposed to be from the hand of Phidias.

A chamberlain swung open the doors and advanced to the table where Clemens sat. "Serene Highness!" he said apologetically, then spoke under his breath. The Elector nodded quickly.

"Yes, yes, bring him in at once. And the banker Hoffman—well, let him wait." Clemens glanced at the two secretaries. "You may go, gentlemen. I'll finish with the dictation later."

After a moment, Count Otto was introduced, and the doors were closed.

With a devout expression and a mincing air, the Count came forward. He bowed low, shook the fine Mechlin lace from his cuffs, and kissed the big amethyst ring of the archbishop-elector. His yellow curls were carefully arranged to conceal a bump and a bit of plaster above his left ear.

"Well, Otto, you're about early. I had no idea you were in the city," Clemens said with a trace of asperity. Perhaps he resented the steel fingers that underlay the silken glove of Osbrock. "I'm surprised that you'd bother to pay your respects to me."

"Your Highness is pleased to jest," Count Otto rejoined. "Your Highness has no more devoted and humbly obedient servant—"

"Yes, yes, I know all that. Save it." Clemens inspected him sharply. "So you call me Highness, not Monseigneur? That

*"Careful!" The word was a croak. "Either I've gone out
of my sense—or we're dealing with Satan in person!"*

means you've come to speak with the Elector, and not with the
Archbishop. Am I correct?"

"The wisdom of Your Highness is omniscient; I have come
to ask for advice," suavely replied the Count. "I have just been
summoned to Berlin on affairs of some moment; before leaving,
I have just handed the treasurer a contribution of ten thousand
ducats toward the expenses of the new Schloss, with my compliments."

"Come! You must be after something worth while this time,"
Clemens made cynical response.

"The advice of Your Highness is more precious than gold—"

"Bah! We're alone; suppose we abandon all pretense," the
Elector broke in. "You care nothing for anyone's advice, Otto.
You serve Frederick of Prussia, not Clemens of Treves. What
are you after now? Let's reach the point."

Count Otto sighed.

"Your Highness is displeased; I regret the fact, but am helpless. I have come to inform Your Highness of the crimes com-
mitted by two French gentlemen in your territories and to seek
your advice. These men are really French agents. They have

seized and abducted a noble lady who was residing quietly in Cologne and have brought her through the territory of Treves, here to Coblenz. They have killed or injured several subjects of Your Highness. Two of my own men were killed by them the day before yesterday."

CLEMENS FROWNED. "What? Are you certain of your facts?"

"Absolutely. One of these men is a Vicomte de St. Denis, a French nobleman of vicious character, who spent several years in the Bastille. The other is a secret agent known as Luther Grimm—"

"What?" exclaimed the Elector. "Why, I know this man Grimm. I have dealt with him. He's a most astute fellow. Not the sort to abduct a young woman."

"It has been done," said Count Otto, and thumbed his little mustache. "This man Grimm is indeed most astute; further, he is rumored to be one of the greatest masters of fence in Europe. At Vienna, a year ago, he gave an exhibition of the sword before the Emperor. Now it appears that his mind is deranged, and he has become criminal."

"If this information is correct, as I assume it to be," the Elector said sharply, "these men must be arrested. I'll not permit such scoundrels to exist in my realm!"

Count Otto bowed. "Not ten minutes ago, Highness, I received sure information where to find this man St. Denis, and no doubt the other with him. He is at the Rittersturtz, a few miles below the city, trying to get across the Rhine. I have given orders which will prevent his escape."

"Without my permission?"

"An emergency, Highness! I hastened here for your advice and counsel. Your Highness is friendly and even allied with France. It might make trouble were these men seized and put to the question, by you."

"It must be done!" Clemens puffed put his cheeks. "Murder, eh? I'll not permit such crimes to go unpunished!"

"Ah, Your Highness is the very soul of justice!" Count Otto said warmly. "Still, expediency is a great thing. It might be better for you to know nothing of what takes place, especially as I hope to catch both these men in the same net. Suppose they were to leave your territory and cross the Rhine. Suppose I, acting on behalf of Prussia, were to conclude the matter fittingly myself? Your Highness would be relieved of all inquiries or responsibility."

The Elector frowned, pursed up his lips, and reflected. He was startled; this was an emergency; and emergencies upset him. It suggested acute trouble with France, and he desired no trouble.

"How," he asked, "would you seize these villains?"

"By sunset they'll be secured. How? By assisting them to escape across the Rhine. They'll disappear from sight."

"Well, I'll have nothing to do with it," decided Clemens abruptly. "Do what you like; I leave it to you. The moment I receive official notice of the matter will be time enough to worry about it."

"The clemency of Your Highness, the prudence, the wisdom, is superb!" Count Otto exclaimed admiringly. "So, with permission, I'll take my leave and follow the counsel so happily received. May God keep Your Highness!"

"Wait!" Clemens checked him. "How did you happen to learn about these men being at the Rittersturtz?"

"Through a secretary of the banker Hoffman. The police inform me that Hoffman acts as French agent and will bear watching—"

"Hoffman is most valuable to me," broke in the Elector, almost angrily. "Let the police spy on him all they like. Of course he's a French agent. However, I do not want him molested or troubled in any way. Look to it!"

Count Otto bowed low, and took his departure after receiving the episcopal, if somewhat mechanical, blessing.

In the anteroom outside he came upon the banker Hoffman;

with him was a bespectacled notary. Count Otto nodded affably to the banker, and went his way.

WHEN THE two had been admitted to the presence of the ruler, Clemens spoke abruptly:

"Who's this man? Oh, I remember. Something about a message from Berlin?"

Grimm, beckoned, came forward and bowed respectfully.

"A message from King Frederick, for your ear alone, Highness. I had the honor of conversing with him last week. He was good enough to entrust me with a few words for you."

Hoffman had already retreated out of earshot. Clemens helped himself copiously to snuff and nodded to the notary. There was no reason to doubt such a message, so sent. Frederick the Great was noted for his eccentricity, for mingling with people of low degree, for abrupt and unconventional ways.

"Well, my man? The message?"

"Highness, these are his exact words: 'If you should see the Elector of Treves, tell him three things for his ear alone. First, he allows himself to be served by a rascal. Second, let him believe nothing that he may hear about the French agent Luther Grimm until it is proved. Third, if he does not cleanse the stables of the Last Virgin, another may do it for him. That is all.'"

CLEMENS REGARDED the notary with startled gaze.

"Eh? The Last Virgin—why, that's Osbrock's inn! Yet Frederick cherishes Osbrock, holds him in high regard…. Hm! A damnably sharp old fellow, Frederick. Served by a rascal, am I? Whom did he mean by that? Not Count Otto?

Grimm bowed again.

"Your Highness undoubtedly understands the message. I do not."

"Hm! Perhaps Osbrock doesn't stand so well with Frederick, after all," mused the Elector. Then he frowned. "If that's a threat, he'd better be careful! Treves is no dependency of Prussia.

Perhaps it's a warning…. Well, well, thank you for the message, my good man. You may go, Hoffman."

The two departed. The carriage of the banker was waiting in the courtyard. As they approached it, one of Hoffman's clerks appeared.

"Master! This message arrived after you had gone. Your secretary opened it, and sent me on with it as being urgent."

Hoffman opened a paper, glanced at it, and turned to Grimm.

"Here. Read it."

Grimm glanced at the writing, which was a huge sprawling scribble: *"Hoffman: If anyone asks for me, I'm waiting at the Rittersturtz. Wonderful wine here. —St. Denis."*

Grimm was for an instant aghast. Hoffman was watching him anxiously, and now spoke under his breath.

"Is it his writing? A strange way for him to reach me."

"His writing, yes." Grimm crushed the message in his hand and pocketed it. "Not his usual writing, though. The fool's drunk. Why didn't he come to you himself? Afraid he might be recognized, perhaps…. Drunk—drunk! Heaven save me from a fool! I'd clear forgotten that St. Denis had that weakness. Well, it's my own fault. What's this place he speaks of, the Rittersturtz?"

"A hill, a tavern, on the river just below the city. If you want to borrow this carriage of mine—"

"Thanks, no. I must go back to my own inn first; I'll walk. We separate here. Thanks for all your assistance. Is there any chance of this message having leaked out through anyone in your office?"

"No," said the banker. "My secretary can be trusted."

"Then—until we meet again!"

Luther Grimm strode out of the palace courtyard with his slight limp, and soon lost himself in the street throngs. The passport and papers of Jan Stern were in his pocket. As he made his way to the Fürstenhof, he recovered from the anger that had seized him. After all, it might be as well that St. Denis had not risked showing his face in the city. But how the devil had St. Denis, drunk or sober, reached the Rittersturtz instead of coming into Coblenz?

"I'll soon learn," thought Grimm, and his spirits rose. "Well, I've put a flea into the Elector's ear that'll keep him interested! And if Luther Grimm shows up here unexpectedly, Clemens won't throw him into a cell on Osbrock's advice."

He purchased a few things of which he had need, exchanged his clumsy stick for a sword-cane with a very fair blade, and so came back to the Fürstenhof. Here he learned that Marie and Jacques had departed, and nodded contentedly. Having paid his score, he engaged one of the carriages at the door and told the driver to take him to the Rittersturtz.

THE CARRIAGE passed the valley of the Laubbach; the driver pointed with his whip to the Rittersturtz ahead—a low hill commanding a glorious view of the river and city with the higher humps of the Dommelberg and the Kuhkopf bulking up behind.

On the hill, as the winding road took them upward, was disclosed a charming old tavern, its grounds laid out with flowers and shrubs. Grimm alighted, dismissed his carriage, and went into the tavern. Noon was approaching, and so he ordered a bottle of wine, a meal, and made inquiries about the Vicomte de St. Denis. No such person was known here.

Considerably relieved by this indication of caution on the part of St. Denis, Grimm went out for a stroll while his meal was preparing. As he came to the end of the gardens, he caught sight of three men talking together. Two of them he took to be peasants or boatmen; the third was St. Denis.

Beyond his change of clothes, the Frenchman had made no attempt at any disguise. He finished his talk with the two men, and they departed. Then St. Denis swung around, glanced at the apparent notary, and without a second look was passing when Grimm spoke to him:

"M. de St. Denis, I believe?"

"Eh?" The Frenchman turned. "Yes, yes. What do you want?"

"I have a message for you," said Grimm in French. "My master says that you made a great mistake in getting drunk last night."

"Diable!" St. Denis stared. "I learned that this morning. My head's still bursting…. Look here, who are you? Who's your master?"

AT THE bewilderment in the man's face, at his sudden suspicion, Grimm exploded in a gust of laughter. He resumed his own normal voice.

"Comrade, you're not so good at this game! Sending that note to Hoffman was a mistake—"

"You! Why, damnation take you, I never suspected it—*you!*" St. Denis seized him in a hearty embrace of wild delight. "You rascal! That note to Hoffman? Well, it's true I had a bit to drink. However, I didn't want to show my face in Coblenz. I got here without coming through the city at all, you see. And the lady?"

"Marie? Oh, she's splendid! She got off for Berlin this morning."

"Good. So you criticize my letter to Hoffman, eh? Let me tell you—"

"Forget it," Grimm intervened. "No harm done; you shouldn't have used your own name. However, you did well not to enter the city without some disguise, for the police are hunting high and low."

"I'm no play-actor," St. Denis growled. "However, all's well. You saw those two men? River men. They have a boat close by, a fine big craft. At sunset they'll put us across, and no questions asked. I didn't have money enough to pay them in full, but you can take care of that."

"Come along. I've ordered a meal. Talk as we eat—no French, remember."

FROM ACROSS the table, St. Denis eyed him curiously.

"Marvelous, Grimm! You've become a different person. I

don't see how you do it! So our Marie has become a man, eh? That girl's an angel, comrade. If I were twenty years younger, I'd—well, I'd take to dreaming."

"Nothing to prevent you," said Grimm.

"Bah! Don't be a fool," broke in St. Denis, with his sardonic twist of the lip. "The Bastille ended me for flights of fancy!"

Before going to the Frenchman's room, Grimm examined the place and everyone in sight before deciding for himself that it was safe to remain here for the afternoon. With his customary attention to detail, he took such things for granted only after he had satisfied his own wary senses.

Alone at last, Grimm abandoned spectacles, wig and pose, and got his pipe out. His money, in gold, was safe in a belt under his clothes. He had kept out only enough for current expenses.

"Did you bargain with those boatmen for one passenger or two?" he inquired.

"Two. I thought you'd be along today," said St. Denis. "So, comrade! All grief has an end. The road's clear now. When I was in the Bastille, I said to myself that it was the end—I'd never crack a smile again. But look at me now! By the way, I was talking last night with the innkeeper here. I mentioned that I'd come from the Last Virgin. He knows Count Otto and got to talking about him—"

"Eh?" Grimm gave him a sharp glance.

St. Denis waved his hand.

"Oh, never fear! He suspected nothing. But he also spoke about the Countess. He hates the two of them like poison. He says that damned woman is worse than a dozen of her husband."

Grimm frowned, shrugged and changed the subject.

"If we finish this errand, I'm coming back to these parts some day," he said. "I want to go through the Inn of the Last Virgin— with about fifty men at my back. I've heard queer rumors about that place, for years past; everyone has."

"I want to go through it with a sword in one hand and a torch in the other," St. Denis added with a growl of oaths. "But when we get around to it, watch out for one man—that fellow they call Master Rudolph, the landlord. He's no fool."

Luther Grimm puffed at his pipe and grinned.

"Neither am I—sometimes. Well, for the present we have the Rhine to cross, and Berlin ahead. Once across, I'll take your disguise in hand and give you a few pointers."

They passed the afternoon in talking, drinking and making plans—plans destined to a sudden and abortive ending.

CHAPTER V

AFOOT, LUTHER Grimm and St. Denis followed the boatman who came to get them. They came down into the wide highway, and went on to a group of buildings by the river's edge, where a large craft lay moored to a wharf. Grimm eyed the road and the dust by the wharf.

"A carriage has been here," he said. The boatman, who was the skipper of their craft, grinned.

"Yes, Excellency. We smuggle over a bit of contraband now and then from Nassau, on the other side of the river. Our customers come to get it by wagon and by carriage…. Will you have some supper before we leave?"

"We've just finished a meal, thanks."

"Then we might as well go aboard and be off. We'll need an hour to get across, as we must pull up against the current to reach our usual landing. Your worships may have the cabin. Now about the payment to be made in advance—"

This detail was quickly settled.

As they went aboard, their guide shouted. Some men came from ashore, others tumbled up from below—ten in all, with the master. Sturdy, cheerful fellows, who loosed the mooring-lines and got out sweeps, five to a side.

The craft, as Grimm noted at a glance, was a decked barge,

"Damn you! Keep away—don't trip him!"

with an after deckhouse or cabin, a mast forward with furled sail, and plenty of cargo-space below.

They went to the cabin. It was large, crudely furnished, and was lit by a stern window of some size which had apparently never been opened. St. Denis settled himself in one of the bunks, but Luther Grimm went back on deck. He stood by the helmsman, as the boat got away.

The men tugged lustily at the long oars, heading the boat upstream along the shallows where the current was not so rapid.

"We'll make that island just this side of the Lahn," said the master, who came to join Grimm. "But to do it, and reach the landing beyond, we must go up higher on this side. The current has a sweep here. It'll be dark long before we land; and so much the better."

Already the level rays of the sun were tipping only the higher hills above the river. The vineyard slopes were merged into the background.

Grimm had carefully kept to his rôle of notary. To his queries, the boatman assured him that horses could be had at the landing, or could be bought at any farm or vineyard near by.

He eyed the opposite shore with a heart well-content. Once they picked up the highway a long road lay ahead, on through Nassau and Hesse and Saxony, through minor states and principalities, with Berlin at the end; swiftest travel of all was by the diligence, for a private carriage would attract too much attention, would be too easily traced....

And at Berlin waited Mortlake, the one-eyed Englishman. Thought of him grew upon Luther Grimm.

Thus he stood musing on the darkling river, until he became aware that the boat had changed course. It was heading across the stream now, the men tugging hard to keep the current from sweeping them too far.

"There's a lantern in the cabin," said the boatman. "I can't spare a man to light it, but your worship will find flint and steel—"

"I have everything," said Grimm.

He went back into the cabin. With St. Denis' tinder-box, he soon had the swinging lantern alight. St. Denis sat up and began to polish Grimm's sword-cane. He looked up at Grimm with a chuckle.

"Comrade, I'd like to meet this sister of our pretty lady—what's her name?"

"Flora."

"Right. I wish she'd make a pass or two at me, as she did at you. I'd reform her quick enough!"

"She'd reform you with a dagger, as she tried to do with me."

"Bah! You red-skinned savages from America don't know how to deal with a fine lady like that. Fine lady, eh? You kiss her hand; what that sort needs is a box on the ear. And if we keep to the main highways, we may run into her. Or perhaps we'll run into Marie."

"Not likely," said Grimm, "but not impossible, either. She may be staying in Coblenz, for all I know. Count Otto, I take it, heads for Berlin; she may go with him or may not. He'll have to patch up his whole cursed intrigue now, with Marie gone. His one chance to catch her and win, is to kill me."

"War to the knife, without quarter, eh?" St. Denis laughed. "I hope you know the country ahead. I don't."

"It's savage enough, in more ways than one. This isn't France we're facing, but Prussia; it's an untamed country. I've been through it more than once. Anything can happen there, and anything does happen."

"So much the better." St. Denis spoke blithely. "This isn't a bad sword you got hold of. I wish I could use the damned thing the way you can! I'll poke my nose on deck for a breath of air. That window apparently doesn't open."

Grimm nodded, stuffed his pipe, and got it alight, while St. Denis started for the deck.

It was still far from dark outside, but evening was rapidly closing down on the river. They must be getting well across by this time, thought Grimm. He puffed his pipe well afire; then, at a step, turned and glanced up. St. Denis had come back.

Grimm stiffened, speechless for an instant. The face of St. Denis was livid; his eyes were bulging; his mouth was opening and closing spasmodically.

"What the devil!" Grimm leaped up.

"Careful!" The word was a croak. St. Denis beckoned. "Either I've gone out of my senses or—or we're dealing with Satan in person. Come and look."

Grimm followed him to the cabin door. St. Denis opened it a couple of inches.

Looking out, Grimm saw that they were nearly across the river. They were, indeed, under the bare little rocky islet the boatman had pointed out to him. Two men up forward were getting ready the landing-ropes. Grimm half turned.

"I don't see anything wrong—"

"Wait!" St. Denis spoke hoarsely, at his ear. "There, he's coming now!"

Ten feet away in the gathering twilight, a figure came into Grimm's range of vision. It was Count Otto—*Count Otto!* Grimm stared, swallowed hard, saw another man come up to the Count and speak—a soldier.

"The men are all up, Highness, and ready."

Luther Grimm softly closed the door. He bolted it, then turned and stared at St. Denis, his brain afire.

I N A flash, he had the explanation: There had been some leak in Hoffman's office. The secretary who had opened that letter? Well, no use upbraiding St. Denis now.

"Caught," he asserted quietly. "Count Otto and his men were below the whole time. It was a trap. The boat—everything."

A contortion passed across the features of St. Denis.

"I see; you were right," he said slowly. "It was that accursed letter with my name in it. I wrote it last night; I was drunk. It didn't need to have my name signed, of course. So it's all my fault, my fault!"

Grimm was paying no heed.

"Stop your babbling. They've waited to spring the trap here, because they mean to finish us and throw us into the river. No quarter! That's it. Well, there's the window. We're across to the shore, it's close. Can you swim?"

St. Denis gaped at him.

"Swim? What do you mean?"

"It's getting darker every minute. Almost too dark to see much of anything now. We can slip away and make the shore before they know it. You can swim?"

"Oh, swim!" St. Denis uttered a hoarse and terrible laugh that held no mirth. "Of course, of course. The Bastille is a great educator; one learns everything there. Or almost everything. I can swim like a fish."

"Then get that rear window open. No time to lose."

They darted to the window, with the lantern. A swift examination showed there was no chance whatever of opening it; the frame was built solidly into place. Luther Grimm lifted his foot and drove it at one of the two panes.

The glass shivered out. Another kick, and he had cleared away most of the jagged fragments about the edge. The rest came away easily, leaving an opening well over a foot square; it was large enough to squeeze through.

Voices sounded outside the door. A heavy knock sounded.

"Go, get off with you!" exclaimed St. Denis quickly. "If you can get those shoulders through, it'll be easy for me."

Grimm stooped. He got his legs through the opening, and worked his body after them. More knocks at the door, imperative voices.

He was through at last, his shoulders scraping clear, his legs hanging. It was a six-foot drop to the water. Gripping the window-edge with his hands, he hung there and glanced up. The rail overhead was silent and deserted; there was no suspicion of this evasion.

"You'll be right along?" he grunted.

St. Denis had come close, his face to the opening, gazing down at Grimm.

"Sorry, comrade!" And his sardonic laugh rang out softly. There was a hammering at the cabin door now, a thudding.

"You should have known that the one trick nobody ever learns in the Bastille—is to swim."

"What?" gasped out Luther Grimm, in sudden frightful realization. "You can't swim? You lied to me?"

"Exactly. It's my fault that we're trapped; I'll pay. You wouldn't have gone if you'd known the truth. But now you have to go. Win the game for us both, comrade! For us, and for the sweet girl. Go with God, my friend—"

Desperately, frantically, Grimm drew himself up. The fist of St. Denis smashed down on the fingers of his right hand; they loosened. He fell, hanging by one hand. One furious oath, one effort to claw up—then St. Denis knuckled his other hand, hammered the fingers, leaned down and thrust at his shoulders. Grimm's hold gave way; he went down, and the water closed over him.

The money-belt of gold about his waist dragged at him. No time, no way to get rid of that burden now. He had to fight for very life, with a horror of despair at his heart. The thought of St. Denis was torment to him.

He struck out desperately as the current gripped him. Breaking the surface, he found himself in shelter of that little rocky islet. Stroking rapidly, he headed for it. The gold, his garments, his boots, weighted him down. Worse yet was the realization that he had no other course. No use blinking the facts; any return to the boat was impossible. It would only be giving himself up to be murdered.

HIS FEET struck shallows. He stumbled on until the water was around his knees. From here across to the Nassau bank was only a little way, a short swim; but he could not go yet. He turned and stared at the barge, scarcely fifty feet distant; an anchor had been put out, and she was swinging on the current.

Her after deck was clearly revealed to him, as two lanterns were held high and cast a flood of light on the cabin doorway. The circling throng of men there had fallen back, well back. Into that doorway Grimm saw St. Denis come, sword-cane in hand, his air cool and collected. Count Otto, flinging aside his coat of silk brocade, bowed to that tall slim figure. St. Denis returned the bow with a low laugh.

GRIMM COULD guess what had happened while he was swimming, from the words that reached him clearly.

"Well, I'm here," said St. Denis. "Are you trying to trick me out of shelter so your men can stab me in the back?"

"Upon my word of honor, I'm hardly so crude." A rapier glinted in the hand of Count Otto. "I face you, and I alone. But where's your friend Grimm?"

"Damned if I know!" exclaimed St. Denis joyously, lightly. "There was a cursed rascally notary with me; he had agreed to put me on the Berlin road—and he went out the stern window with all my money. I believe that Grimm is by this time well on his way to Berlin."

"So? A likely story, but I hardly credit it," Count Otto rejoined smoothly. "So I must first attend to you, then to him, eh? Very well. Surely you're not afraid to meet my poor rapier?"

"Devil take me if I ask anything better!" cried St. Denis, and flung himself forward.

Steel glittered in the lantern light, glittered and crossed, clashed. Watching, Grimm caught his breath with fear, with hope, with wild anxious suspense. After all, St. Denis was a splendid blade. He himself had taught the man a world of skill with—

Ah! St. Denis was down! Up again on the instant; up again, a little splotch of scarlet growing on his shirt. Too confident, eh? No great hurt; a mere touch. He was laughing now, laughing and thrusting in. Grimm stiffened. Good God, what an attack! No swordsman could stand before that dazzling assault!

Count Otto stood before it; not only stood, but returned thrust for thrust, an agile and amazing figure to see. The two blades clung in the air, grated, disengaged, rippled in and out faster than eye could follow. Minutes dragged on.

Suddenly a cry broke from the men. Count Otto staggered

back a pace or two. His right sleeve darkened; blood dripped over his hand and fingers. Swift as light, his rapier glinted as he tossed it to his left hand. Rapidly, fiercely, he pressed in with so terrible an attack that St. Denis was forced back and back.

The lean dark man hardened. Now his thin sliver of steel became a flashing wall through which no thrust or riposte could pierce. He gave attack for attack. Luther Grimm, looking with every nerve tense, realized that St. Denis was exerting a super-human skill in this moment—

"Damn you! Keep away from him—don't dare trip him!"

The sharp, furious cry broke from Count Otto, as though at some man behind St. Denis; but there was none behind him. The Frenchman flung a startled glance over his shoulder; and in this instant the Count lunged.

One sharp, frightful oath escaped Grimm as he saw St. Denis go down to that foul thrust. The circle of men closed in. Steel flashed once more, and once more drove to the mark.

"Good luck, comrade—"

The words, bursting from St. Denis, ended in death.

SHIVERING AS from an ague, Grimm wakened from the trance of horror and despair that had gripped him. The boat that was put over from the deck of the barge was already filling with men. Count Otto was shrilling out orders. Men passed down a lantern to the boat.

Grimm turned and stumbled away with tears on his cheeks, tears of grief and wild fury. Away through the shallows, into the channel, striking out for the shore beyond as he came to deep water.

St. Denis was dead, and had died to save him. And he, weaponless, helpless, futile, could do nothing.

St. Denis dead—and tricked into death! This thought burned like very insanity within him, spurring him into frantic efforts that he could not even realize. The weight of the gold bore him down anew, as he headed for shore.

From the boat issued a chorus of excited shouts. The men in it found his floating hat and wig; the hue and cry redoubled as they pressed on in hot pursuit of him.

CHAPTER VI

GRIMM DRAGGED himself ashore gasping, agonized, ignorant of what lay ahead. In those frenzied efforts to claw back up to the stern window of the boat, he had hurt himself—had twisted his muscles, reviving the pain of those long searing bayonet-wounds that had ended his soldiering back in America. He was in agony of body and mind alike.

The passing of this frightful night remained to him afterward as the memory of blind and shivering horror. Everywhere were bobbing lanterns as men searched for him. He struggled desperately to find his way somewhere, and could not. By a miracle,

he evaded all pursuit, crawling into coverts, getting a snatch of sleep here and another there. Sometime after midnight, dragging himself through a vineyard, he discerned the dark mass of a house ahead. Dogs rushed out at him. He was beating them off frantically when a woman appeared with a lantern, had a glimpse of him, and uttered a piercing shriek.

"The devil is in the vineyard, Hans! The devil is in the vineyard!" rang out her wild cries.

Grimm fled, rid himself of the dogs, and stumbled on, his whole body an ache.

Dawn was touching the east with gray when he came at last

to a hill road and followed it blindly. Here, as it proved, luck was with him. Day was breaking, the golden spears of sunrise were lifting from the horizon, when he finally realized that he had come into a broad highroad. This was the highway that led to Ems and on to distant Berlin.

Sobbing relief shook his exhausted frame, and he cursed the ague of the Jersey marshes that shook him intolerably. That immersion, that burst of desperate effort, had wakened all the old ills. He was a walking scarecrow, his shrunken garments still soggy, the weight of gold still about his waist as he staggered on.

He could do no more. He sank down on a rock beside the road. Removing some of his sodden garments, he waited for the genial sunrise to dry and warm him. Chills shook him repeatedly, and there was a dry burning in his head.

The sound of hoof-beats roused him to sunlight; his dull eyes lifted, focused—and he knew he was lost. His head fell.

Two horsemen were swinging along the road, only to draw rein and stare hard at him. No help here. These were soldiers; and in one of them he recognized the man he had glimpsed on the barge, the man who had spoken to Count Otto.

Hurriedly they dismounted and rushed toward him. Grimm could not move.

"It's the man himself, the very man!" exclaimed one of the two. "We've found him! Remember the orders. Bring him in not alive, but dead."

"Make sure of him first," grunted the second. Leaning over, he caught Grimm by the shoulder and shook him savagely. "Wake up, fellow! Who are you and where from? Answer!"

Luther Grimm's eyes swept them, swept on to the horses with their holstered pistols. A spark came afire in his brain and he came lurching and staggering to his feet, putting a hand to his pocket. He drew out a fistful of gold.

"Here, take it," he mumbled, and flung the coins into the dust.

With a sharp cry one of the two men darted on the glittering coins. Grimm broke from the other, and flung himself
forward in one last effort of brain and muscles, one convulsive
burst of energy. The man whipped out sword and came leaping
after him.

Already Grimm was at the horses, however, snatching the
pistol from the nearest holster. He swung around. If the priming
was wet, if it missed fire—

The heavy pistol roared, spurted smoke, and the soldier
plunged forward on his face; his sword rattled at Grimm's feet.
The second man was already running forward with a yell of
dismay and rage.

Grimm stooped, swept up the fallen sword, and steadied
himself. He met the attack with a sudden access of strength
and fury. Here was one, at least, who had helped St. Denis to
die!

This soldier knew his business; but Luther Grimm, despite
his fevered brain, knew it better. At the third pass he ran the
man through, and stepped back.

"No foul blow there," he panted harshly. "And no trick,
either!"

The soldier crumpled to the ground, cursing. Grimm dragged
the two bodies off the road. A sword at his hip, a horse to ride….
Again he was on his way.

O N T H E outskirts of Ems, Grimm turned the horse loose
and went afoot into the little town. He had scarcely put down
a flagon of wine at the post tavern, when the diligence from
Coblenz came roaring in with a blare of post-horns. Grimm
had just time to secure a place and scramble aboard.

Despite the fearful jolting, he soon fell into a doze that lasted
for hours, though with frequent breaks. The thought of Mortlake filled his flittering mind.

At noon he came awake with fever-fancies dancing through
his head, with alternate burnings and chills seizing him, with
visions of St. Denis and Mortlake still pursuing his wild

thoughts. Only by a frightful effort could he keep himself from talking aloud, from muttering wild words.

It was toward sunset when the diligence rattled into Altendorf, with Coblenz now far away and forgotten over the horizon.

Here there was a wait of fifteen minutes, to change horses and give the passengers a chance at food and drink. Grimm staggered into the tavern room and called for wine. He gulped it from the bottle.

The town was small, but the place was full of people, the inn yard held several coaches and carriages. To Grimm, everything was a blur. He had lost coherence.

Then, suddenly, one thing came clear: the face of a man in the street, passing the tavern. A face with one eye gone, the other alive and flaming. He could see the man there in the street, a massive figure swinging along. Mortlake! One wild yell burst from Grimm.

Like a man drunk,—as in fact he was,—Luther Grimm hurled himself out of the tavern, tugging at his sword. He swiftly over-took that heavy figure. The man turned a broad, honest face to him in startled amazement and fear. To Grimm's fevered vision it was the face of Mortlake, and he came in with his blade lunging.

The hapless man evaded the wild attack and shouted frantically for help. Townsfolk came running. Burghers and apprentices came leaping to quell the shouting madman.

A furious commotion arose, as Grimm found himself beset and began to fight everyone in sight. The whip of a carter

"You don't appear to recognize your dear sister, Flora," went on Marie, acid in her voice. "What a charming conversation I've interrupted!"

curled about Grimm's sword, wrenching it from his grasp. The tumult grew.

A wooden *sabot* was hurled. It caught Grimm over the eyes and knocked him backward on the stones. Men piled on him. Bare-handed, he won free of them, fighting desperately. Some one tripped him, and he was down again.

Even so, he still fought with spasmodic fury. The crowd jammed the street and choked the tavern entrance. Blows were showered on the writhing, struggling figure, blood was running down his cheek. Suddenly he collapsed in utter exhaustion and fell forward on his face. He lay quiet, except for his rasping breath.

The burgomaster came shoving through the yelling throng. Place was made for him. He surveyed Luther Grimm and stroked his beard, and shook his head.

"A lunatic, a madman," he said pityingly. "Bring chains. Rivet them on his arms and legs, and put him into the jail—"

"Your pardon, Burgomaster," intervened a soft voice. "I know the man. Let me beseech you to place him in my charge. He's not mad; rather, he's ill. He evidently has fever. Turn him over to me, and I'll be responsible for him."

CHAPTER VII

LUTHER GRIMM vaguely remembered that attack of frenzy, as in the wasting memory of dream; it seemed like a part of that fever-ridden nightmare of wandering, with the dying words of St. Denis following him like a pursuing ghost. Then came faint recollections—the face of Marie bending over him and her voice in his ears, the jolting of a cushioned carriage, a cooling drink.

The slight echoes lingered in his brain when he came definitely awake to warm sunlight and voices, coherent impressions. He felt perfectly clear in his mind, but devilish hungry and thirsty. He turned his head and looked around curiously. He was lying in bed, beside wide open windows, in an empty room—a room in some tavern, by its looks.

I T W A S early morning. Close by, outside his windows, level sunbeams fell upon two grooms washing a carriage; a third man was sauntering toward the two and engaging them in conversation. Grimm found himself staring hard at this third man, whose wrinkled features snatched at his memory. Bits of talk drifted to him from the three.

"Whose carriage?" One of the grooms laughed. "It belongs to the lady who came in yesterday afternoon. How should I know her name?"

The third man shrugged and turned. He came past the windows. On abrupt and sharp impulse, Grimm lifted himself to one elbow.

"Jacques!" his voice rang out. "Is it really you?"

The dried-up old servitor of Courland—yes, no other! He started, glanced around and caught sight of Grimm's face. He stared with fallen jaw and a look of utter stupefaction; then he swung around and fairly ran from Grimm's vision.

With an oath of puzzled astonishment, Luther Grimm tried to get to the window. Grimacing, he fell back on the pillows. He was stiff and sore; plaster hid a cut on his forehead; his entire body ached with bruises, cuts, contusions. Dimly he recalled that fracas in the street of Altendorf. Where was he now? He had encountered Marie, of course, or she must have found him and taken care of him. Then why that look of amazement on the face of her servant? It was all most bewildering.

The door of the room opened. He looked around to see a serving-maid of the inn, holding a tray. She came forward, smiling cheerfully at him.

"How did I get here?" Grimm demanded abruptly.

"In a carriage, of course!" She laughed as she set down the tray.

"But where am I—what town is this?"

A furious
commotion arose,
as Grimm found
himself beset, and
began to fight
everyone in sight.

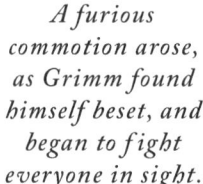

"You're in bed," she replied gayly. "This is Dortstadt, sir, the finest town in all Saxony. I'll tell Madame that you're awake."

She went out hastily. Saxony! Then, thought Grimm, he was already far on the way to Berlin—but how the devil had he got here? Madame? That would be Marie, no doubt. Then what had become of Mortlake?

Grimm shoved perplexity aside and attacked the food ravenously. In the midst, the memory of St. Denis smote him like an actual blow…. Dead, and tricked into death!

The thought was like the impact of a spur, goading him out of bed. His clothes, or rather the garments he had worn, lay on a chair at one side. He staggered to them, struggled painfully into them; the effort left him weak and sick with the hurt of his bruised body, for the fever had robbed him of strength.

Presently he was able to finish his breakfast, and the aching

muscles gradually relaxed until he could move more naturally. His papers and money were gone. He had no weapon.

There was a step, a hand at the door; it swung open. Grimm leaped to his feet with a glad word.

"Marie! Then it was you after all—"

"It was I, yes; but not Marie."

Smiling, she came to him as he stood stunned—partly by realization of the truth, partly by the sheer glorious beauty of her. At this early morning hour her loveliness was a sheer miracle.

She was gowned in rich blue velvet sewn with seed-pearls. Her pale golden hair was like an aureole about her features. So warm and aglow with friendliness was her face, so merry and sparkling, that Grimm was dumfounded. He could not believe that this was the woman who, at their last remembered meeting, had come at him with a poniard.

She held out her hand to him with a frank and winning air.

"A lucky thing for you that I happened to pass and recognize you, night before last, or you'd be in a lunatic's cell this minute! Come—will you forgive me for all that happened when we last met? It's easy to make mistakes, you know; especially when one has been the victim of outrageous lies. But now I've learned the truth about that man."

Luther Grimm took her hand and bowed over it. He met her steady gaze, his own eyes edged with surmise.

"What man?"

She shivered slightly, and her reply all but stupefied him.

"My husband—Otto. And all the while I thought that you had entrapped my poor sister, that you were forcing her to do as you desired, that you—oh, it was all so horrible! I tried to beguile you; I would gladly have killed you, for her sake; but now I know the truth. And I'm ashamed."

"Then it's to you I owe my life and safety?" Grimm asked slowly.

"And health, thanks to my knowledge of herbs and drugs." Under the open admiration of his regard, she smiled again. "Oh, you owe me nothing, really! I'm the one who am in debt, my friend."

Grimm smiled dryly. "True, perhaps. My money's gone—"

"All safe." Laughing, she turned and pointed at a little leather bag in one corner. "I put your papers and money in that bag, for convenience. So much gold would be a sore temptation to servants. Come along, let's see if it's safe."

She tugged at his hand and led him over to the corner. He lifted the bag to the table and opened it. Loose gold, inside, and the papers of Jan Stern.

"Are you satisfied?" she demanded, looking into his face. Grimm shook his head slightly and frowned.

"No. What do you intend? What's the reason of this friendship?"

A WARMTH of sympathy flooded her face. She laid a hand on his arm, and met his gaze with so earnest, so appealing an expression that for a moment he was shaken.

"You've every right to suspect me; but now I've been able to prove my good will toward you," she said quietly. "Forget all the lies that have been told about me, as I've forgotten those told me about you. I can give you all you desire, and more. I can help you and help Marie, now that I know all the truth. I can open all doors to you, show you secrets, wealth, other things at Otto's castle and at the Last Virgin, that will astonish you. I can help you to whatever you want in this world—"

He listened with only idle attention to her words. He was reflecting swiftly on what lay behind them. At the moment he was no beauty, and he knew it. She certainly was not attracted by any appeal in his looks. By what, then? Hard to say, just now.

"Where's Count Otto?" he asked abruptly.

"I don't know. I haven't seen him since we reached Coblenz."

"But I have," said Grimm.

His eyes were not pleasant. She shrank from his gaze, dropped her hand from his arm, and stood with nostrils quivering, breath coming fast. She could not mistake what lay behind those coldly piercing eyes, those coldly significant words.

"SUPPOSE WE abandon pretense, madam," went on Grimm calmly. "For after all, I do owe you much; and whatever your motives, I'm keenly grateful. I'm not your dupe; neither am I your enemy. Will you believe this? You're too beautiful, too intelligent, too wise," he added, his deep blue eyes warming, "to make an enemy of a man who bears you only gratitude."

She bit her lip. The storm passed out of her face.

"But you're a magician!" she murmured. "Indeed, I could almost believe that you're an honest man!"

Luther Grimm smiled. "At times, perhaps; this is one of the times. Will you tell me why you saved my life?"

Under his gaze, her manner changed abruptly. Her voice chilled. A shrewdness, a hardness, glittered in her eyes. Here was a flash of the real woman, unscrupulous, scheming, clever.

"Yes!" she broke out impulsively. "Otto has made a mess of everything, and will listen to no advice. I distrust that man Mortlake; I fear him. Otto is endangering himself and his position, everything! What's more, he's afraid of you. I've never before known him to be afraid of anyone. You're more valuable than he is—"

Luther Grimm broke into a gust of laughter. A month previously, he might have welcomed such an intrigue as was now offered him; but no longer.

"I understand," he cut in with a chuckle. "As a business proposition I'm a better bet than your husband, eh? Madam, I agree with you entirely." He sobered suddenly and bent a quick look upon her. "I'll make you a proposal: Abandon the sinking ship of deceit and crime and intrigue. Throw over this husband of yours, since you pretend to be displeased with him. Just what you're driving at, I don't know or care, but I'll accept you at face value. Help your sister to get her inheritance. Throw your energy and ability on the side of right and justice. I'll lend you a hand with this—"

Her eyes blazed at him with incredulous scorn, disdain, contempt.

"Do you dare to mock me?" she burst out passionately.

"God forbid!" said Luther Grimm, intent and grave. "I give you the advice of an honest man."

A low, musical laugh rang upon the room.

"As if she could comprehend such advice, or such a man!" said a new voice.

Grimm swung around. Standing in the doorway was a cloaked figure. In a flash, he recalled and understood the astonishment of old Jacques, the latter's questions about the carriage that was being washed—Flora's carriage—and the departure of Jacques at a run.

"You don't appear to recognize your dear sister, Flora," went on Marie with acid in her voice. "What a charming conversation I've interrupted! But I'll relieve you of Herr Grimm now. I think he travels on to Berlin with me. Comrade, the carriage is ready."

One piercing cry escaped the Countess. Only by the voice, obviously, did she recognize her sister. In this gallant's attire, with wide plumed hat, with the cloak that enveloped her, Marie was past any casual recognition, even as a woman.

"Why—why, you vixen!" gasped out Flora. "You—you damned little trull—"

She took one step toward Marie, with a burst of invective that was terrific; it spared neither oaths nor names. Every vestige of the woman's loveliness took flight before the outbreak of fury that possessed her. In the midst, she hesitated and swayed, uttered a choking gasp, and sank to the floor. This sudden access of hatred, of amazement, of rage and chagrin, had flung her into a dead faint.

"Leave her alone," said Marie calmly. "It will pass. She's subject to such spells of fainting whenever she flies into a fury of emotion. Perhaps it's better so; we can safely leave her. She'll come around in a few moments."

IN ALMOST frantic relief, Grimm caught up the little handbag. He pushed Marie out of the room, closed the door, and turned to her.

"Right! Get out of here in a hurry. Your carriage is here?"

"Yes. It's safe enough, and I've hired one. The Prussian border's just ahead. I tried traveling in the diligence, but it's been crowded, and twice we've been unable to get places. We've lost more time than we've gained."

Her voice was cold, as they hurried together toward the courtyard. She went on even more coldly:

"So she's beautiful, intelligent, wise, is she? And affectionate too, no doubt. Are you sure you wouldn't prefer to go on with her and leave me?"

"Don't be a fool," snapped Luther Grimm angrily. "You had no business revealing yourself to her. You're in the utmost danger, whether here or in Berlin. Count Otto will know exactly whom to look for, now. You've made things doubly hard for us all by this—"

"You certainly don't think me intelligent, do you?" she broke in cuttingly. "Well, don't imagine to yourself that I'm afraid of her. I couldn't miss the chance to face her. I'm only sorry I didn't tell her exactly what I think of her."

"Yes, you would be. All you women are alike," Grimm replied in gusty wrath. Jacques was awaiting them on the box of the carriage. A groom was holding open the door as they approached. "Risking everything to vent your spite and temper; even telling her we're bound for Berlin—why, it's inconceivable! Such folly is past belief."

"You're tremendously grateful to her, aren't you? You owe her your life. You'll not forget it—why, you fool, do you know she's already sent one of her men to the police headquarters here?"

Marie paused on the carriage step, to fling the vehement words into his face. She went on even more heatedly:

"If you'd had sense enough to spar for time, pretend, play the game with her, all might be well; but no! You had to be an honest man, because she's so beautiful! She wasn't taking any chances. She was prepared to make a dupe of you or else put you in safety—to play her own game, or that of Count Otto. In another half-hour you'd have been behind the bars for your fine honesty— Oh, get in, get in and stop your cursing! We've no time to lose here."

Grimm obeyed, with the sickening realization that her argument was sound.

The carriage went leaping away with a jerk. It flung him into the seat opposite Marie; the shock sent a shower of sparks through his head, a spasm of pain through his bruised body.

*Frederick paid no
attention until he had
finished the selection
he was playing.*

White and faint, unable to speak or move, he could only sit there staring at her.

She divined something amiss. Sudden alarm sprang in her eyes; she leaned forward and touched his arm.

"What is it, what's wrong? Why, you're hurt! That cut on your head—how did you get here with her? Why do you owe her your life?" Cutting short her own flood of questions, she reached for a basket that was beneath the seat. "Here, don't speak; take this wine. Drink it."

Grimm took the bottle of wine she thrust at him. As the carriage rattled over the stones of the town streets, he gulped from the bottle. Suddenly he was amazed to find her laughing gayly.

"Aren't people funny when they lose their tempers, comrade? I'm like all damned women; you're a fool—oh, it was a good lively spat!" Her silvery laugh rang out afresh. "I like you when you're angry, Luther Grimm. And really, I must have been terribly unjust. But tell me what's happened since I saw you. Where's St. Denis?"'"

"Dead," Grimm rejoined, and saw the word bring pallor to her cheeks.

HE LEANED back wearily, thankful for the cushions behind him. Almost grudgingly he found himself liking her attitude, her quick flare of temper, her equally quick laughter and apologies. He liked her balance. In the man's attire she wore, it was not so easy to think of her as a woman, as the girl he had known. But the softness of her hand, as it clutched and pressed his own, was most comforting testimony to the fact.

"Oh, my dear man! Really dead? It can't be possible; he was so alive!" Her voice was rich with grief and sympathy. "Tell me how it happened, all of it."

They were past the city gates now and out on the open highway, the horses speeding, the carriage lurching and swaying. Jacques drove as though the devil were after him, and the devil a woman.

So, as they drove on, she heard all the story.

The mere telling of it, facing the repetition of everything, took toll. Luther Grimm, his vitality exhausted, was at low ebb; he sank lower and lower in the grip of despondency and bitterness. He was really appalled by the appearance of Marie before her sister, and by what she had revealed to that woman; it threatened to dash all his plans to bits.

"THE WHOLE thing looks useless," he concluded, with a despairing gesture. "The odds are too heavy. Count Otto controls the police; we're running smack into a trap. Even if you should reach Berlin, what then? Insuperable odds, the most frightful danger on all sides. I don't see any hope for success."

She was white to the lips as she looked at him and listened to his words.

"What do you mean? Is it my presence, the fact that Flora now knows how I'm disguised, that threatens everything?"

"No. The death of St. Denis has opened my eyes. It's a losing game all around," he said gloomily. "They've all the advantage; they hit too hard. It's hard to fight against murder."

He closed his eyes in listless lethargy. Nothing stirred him. Franklin? That old man was far away in Paris. Even farther, over a horizon of dream, lay the armies of Washington and the Continental Congress; a savage laugh stirred in his brain. What mattered his own people, all the driving urge that had spurred him formerly? Nothing. He was pursuing a trail of folly here in Germany. It was impossible, impossible!

He thought briefly of this girl beside him. A little stir wakened in him. After all, she was the one most immediately concerned. She was worth all effort, all the effort possible. A woman depending wholly upon him—well, the more fool she! His mental horizon clouded. A frightful despondency gripped him utterly. The immediate present, the facts facing him, loomed large and terrible.

What use fighting for his own people across the sea? None. It was all quite useless. His father, starving with Washington; his brothers, doomed; his mother and sister, facing an unknown, perilous existence—everything was hopeless. He had cherished such hot and high thoughts of helping them, of doing that which would mean everything to them and other people like them—and it was all folly. He had entered into a game of relentless fury, with odds against which he could not cope. An empty-handed player cannot win.

Then he was aware of her voice, low and grave.

"You're right. You've lost heart, and I don't blame you. At Berlin we may meet disaster. Count Otto is perhaps there already. He travels night and day, goes like the wind, turns up where least expected, winds kings and ministers about his finger. And he has Mortlake to help him—one devil to help another."

"Mortlake!" Grimm's eyes opened.

"And you've no one, now St. Denis is gone."

A flicker came into those deep blue eyes of his. The harsh lines of his features seemed to tighten, become more hawklike.

"Hm! That's something must be paid for, yes. Hello! What's this?"

The carriage had swung out of the highway and halted. They had come to a crossroads, and now Jacques was climbing down to read the half-defaced signposts. Marie answered his question.

"My charming sister will follow the highway. Also, it'll be dangerous for us. I've ordered Jacques to circle around. It's farther, but safer."

"Yes, you're not safe any longer, now that she knows your disguise."

"I'm not safe against lies, treachery, cunning traps—nor against despair," she said quietly, watching him. "Nor against speed. Horses are scarce in Prussia. We can ask for fresh horses, pay for them—and perhaps not get them at all. Otto and my sister can command and take them, every post of twelve miles; running them full gallop between posts, killing them if necessary."

Grimm frowned. He opened the door and climbed out. Jacques was having trouble reading the signposts, and Grimm joined him. Yes, this cross-road would take them on the circuit they desired.

AS THEY stood in discussion, a flare of dust rose on the highway ahead. A courier, perhaps, coming from Berlin. The horseman drew into sight, bore down upon them full gallop. As he thundered past, Grimm heard a startled cry break from him, saw him pulling down his horse.

He halted the beast and came trotting back. His voice lifted.

"Monsieur! Monsieur Grimm!"

"Sainterre, of all people!" Grimm recognized him instantly. One of the secretaries of the Marquis d'Evrecourt, the ambassador to Berlin—a man whom he knew well, and who knew him and his work. Sainterre drew rein, leaned down to shake hands.

"Upon my word, M. Grimm, you're the last person I expected to see!" he exclaimed. "We've been expecting you at Berlin; letters from M. de Vergennes have been awaiting you. I could not help stopping to give you some information. I'm riding for Paris, you see. There wasn't a courier to be had, and Evrecourt sent me."

He glanced at Jacques. Grimm sent the old servitor back to the carriage and gave Sainterre a look.

"Well? What is it?"

"War's threatened," said the other rapidly. "Looks like a certainty. You know, the Elector of Bavaria died without issue. Austria is occupying Bavaria; the Emperor claims Bavaria as his inheritance. King Frederick refuses to recognize it and has sent the Emperor an ultimatum."

GRIMM WHISTLED. "The devil! I understood that Frederick was considering an English alliance!"

"Yes. That devil Mortlake's in Berlin and at work; but now things have changed. It's a question whether Frederick will have more to gain from making war on us, or on Austria. Well, I must be off. I took the opportunity to inform you. I tell you, we need you in Berlin! *Adieu.*"

With a wave of his hand, Sainterre wheeled his horse, spurred the animal into speed, and was gone on a trail of dust.

Grimm hastened back to the carriage, told Jacques to go ahead on the side road, and got in. He swiftly told Marie what he had just learned.

"That's chance for you," he said. "The first sign of luck coming our way! If it had been a courier instead of Sainterre, who knows me well, he wouldn't have stopped. You see what this means?"

She frowned thoughtfully as the carriage jolted into speed.

"Better than you, perhaps," she rejoined. "It means that my money may be the deciding factor, especially with the grasping Frederick. It means that Count Otto and Mortlake can still win everything, if my inheritance is flung into the balance. To catch me, they have only to watch those two bankers, whom I must reach. Oh, I was horribly foolish to let Flora know so much! Now she'll get word there ahead of us. If they do catch me, if it comes to the point of imprisonment and torture, I'll give up the money quickly enough, I fear."

"Frederick wouldn't use torture with a woman."

"Others would. Besides, there's more to it." She kindled quickly. "Don't you think Vienna is moving heaven and earth to throw Frederick against France, backing Count Otto and Mortlake with money and help of every kind?"

Luther Grimm nodded. Yes, she was right. If Frederick went into that English alliance and flung his armies against France, Austria could do as she liked; and it would mean disaster for France, disaster for the Continental armies across the ocean. Washington would get none of the supplies and men and money old Franklin was so desperately trying to secure for him.

"More odds against us," said Grimm. "By heaven, we're fighting all Europe!"

"And the weakness of despair."

He gave the girl a swift smile.

"Perhaps I have my dark moments, comrade, but cheer up. We're not licked yet. Three or four days more will see us in Berlin."

"Where Flora may be ahead of us."

GRIMM LAUGHED. His spirits were reviving; this unexpected news had pulled him back into the game. And this woman, this girl opposite—why, she could bring the dead to life! He was fighting for her too; she had his promise. She was the one who faced the most bitter peril at Berlin.

"Never mind about that woman; you overrate her. We may never see her again."

Marie only smiled in response—a skeptic, pitying smile. Presently she spoke.

"Enjoy your illusions, comrade. It suited her to save you; she has crafty skill with herbs and drugs, and for once she put it to good use. Don't expect her to repeat. Well, forget her!"

"And remember St. Denis," said Grimm, a sudden glitter in his blue eyes.

A good comrade, this Marie! With man's attire, she had donned man's viewpoint, man's attitude, even man's oaths upon occasion. Her quiet argument, Grimm realized, had helped to spur him out of his gloomy despair and prick him back to normal. As the day lengthened and waned, as the present swallowed up the past, he felt more like his old self.

Evening found them across the Prussian border, in a sedate little town. Here Luther Grimm went foraging, with broad gold-pieces to further his aims.

WITH MORNING, a new Grimm swaggered into the inn room to join Marie at breakfast. Her face changed; her eyes grew wide at sight of him: gold-laced coat, brocaded waistcoat, the finest of linen and lace, a rapier at his thigh, and a curled wig framing his lean shaven cheeks.

"Why, Flora was right! You're indeed a magician!" Marie exclaimed delightedly. "How on earth did you get those clothes to fit you, overnight?"

"Like this." Grimm jingled the coins in his pocket.

"Your gold? Or St. Denis' gold?"

An oath came to his lips, as the sting of the words hit him. He looked at her for a moment, then nodded quietly.

"You needn't use the spur any more. I'm myself."

"Thank heaven for that!" She extended her hand to him. "Comrades again?"

"Never anything else, I trust." Grimm's eyes kindled as he returned the clasp of her slim fingers. "And I like you as I first saw you, better than now. When do you get rid of this man's attire?"

"Is it safe to do so?"

He shrugged. "Flora will be ahead of us, or send word; now

your disguise becomes a peril. They won't be looking for a duchess, however—so be one! That's the safest thing, just now."

"But I'm not a duchess, remember! My father's title has been given elsewhere. I'm just Marie of Courland. Very well, then; I'll need a little time and some clothes to return to myself. We should reach Wittenberg early tomorrow afternoon. Shall we stop there, instead of pressing ahead? If you don't mind delays, that is. I must rid my hair of this dye, get clothes, everything!"

"He who delays, runs risk of the devil, as the proverb says." Grimm laughed a little. "But perhaps it'll be best. After all, if King Frederick sees you in your real person, he can deny you nothing. So it's agreed. We'll pause at Wittenberg, then, and bring Marie of Courland back to life."

CHAPTER VIII

I N   B E R L I N a man with one eye stood waiting in the courtyard of the King's residence, Sans Souci. Not the palace of this name, but the retired mansion which Frederick the Great, in the parsimony and eccentricity of his old age, preferred to any palace.

The man in the courtyard was powerfully built. His features expressed great strength, determination and placid poise. The one lost eye did not disfigure him; the lid was closed, that was all, and it merely gave his face a queerly unbalanced look. The one live eye was calm, inscrutable, but between the iris and the lower lid showed a rim of white eyeball; a sure sign of ruthless cruelty.

This man was well dressed. He displayed an air of perfect poise, neither walking nor moving about, but waiting calmly. The dinner hour was just over. No sentries were here; the place seemed empty and deserted, except for a lackey in frayed livery who stood by the entrance door. This lackey presently spoke to the one-eyed man.

"Monsieur, you're having a long wait," he said in French, the official language of the court. Frederick detested his natal tongue. "Don't you want to come into the shade? The sun's hot."

"I'm used to long waits," replied the man calmly. "The longer they are, the better they end."

This air of cool rebuff, this imperturbable sang-froid, disgusted the friendly lackey, who produced a snuffbox and sniffed copiously. Time dragged on.

A ringing click of hoofs, and a carriage appeared, rolling into the courtyard. The lackey sprang to attention. Count Otto von Osbrock alighted, saw the one-eyed man, and beckoned him. Count Otto was magnificently attired in pale blue and silver, and his handkerchief was of the finest lace.

"Ah, Mortlake!" he said affably. "I was delayed by news which will interest you. No time to discuss it now. Are you sure of yourself, in case the King questions you closely?"

A smile, as though of derision, twitched at Mortlake's lips.

"Have you nothing more important to worry about?" he asked.

"Perhaps I have." Count Otto smiled sweetly and thumbed his little yellow mustache. He turned to the lackey. "His Majesty is here?"

"Yes, M. le Comte. But as you know, he always plays the flute after dinner and does not wish to be disturbed."

"I'll announce myself; open the door. Come, Mortlake!"

He entered the house with Mortlake.

Frederick, who played the flute uncommonly well, was alone in a music-room. He wore a distinctly untidy dressing-gown; his wig was awry; his wrinkled and choleric features were intent as he puffed; his large, brilliant eyes were gripped to the music on the rack.

Although he heard some one enter, he paid no attention until he had finished the selection he was playing. Then he swung around in hot anger.

"Haven't I given orders— Oh, it's you, Otto! And when did you return to Berlin?"

"Ten minutes ago, sire." The Count advanced. "I have information of such a character that I came straight to Your Majesty with it. I didn't have the heart to interrupt so lovely an aria, however. I've seldom heard music so well suited to the talent of the artist."

"Humph! A lot you know about music," sniffed the King, but obviously pleased none the less. "Yes, I wrote that aria myself. Well, well, what's your news? I ordered you to produce some proof of your outrageous charges against these French agents, in the Courland matter, and you prate about news!"

"My news, sire, is the proof in question."

Count Otto bowed, produced a snuffbox, and proffered it. The King stuffed a copious helping into each nostril.

"Spanish snuff; you're learning good taste, I see. That is, in some respects." He eyed the gorgeous blue and silver garments with caustic eye. "Come! This Marie of Courland disappeared. You and your wife undertook to find her; you made vague charges of a plot on the part of France and her agents. A hundred millions should have come into my pockets. You promised much; you've produced nothing. Meantime, the Austrians are occupying Bavaria."

"So I have heard," Otto admitted. "As to my poor sister-in-law, I have learned everything. It appears that two French agents were responsible for her disappearance. They clapped her into a convent cell in Cologne on pretense that she was insane. They attempted to force her into signing away her inheritance; finding this legally impossible, they persuaded her to come to Berlin and get it, in their company. They have offered her the protection of France, who in return will take half her patrimony—the half that should go to Your Majesty."

FREDERICK LISTENED, a rising tide of color in his wrinkled cheeks.

"A damned outrage! France, you say, was responsible? Who are these two men?"

"Of course, France would disavow their guilt," suavely said

*"You're the last person I
expected to see, Mr. Grimm!"*

the Count. "You know one of the two, I think; a man named
Grimm—Luther Grimm."

"Grimm? I've heard of the fellow! Said to be a most unusual
agent. Hm! He's playing a bold game for a high stake, eh?"

"Quite so, sire. The other man is—or was—the Vicomte de
St. Denis. In rescuing my sister-in-law from their clutches, I
myself killed St. Denis. The man Grimm escaped us, and took
the poor girl with him. I regret to tell you, sire, that her mind
seems to have become deranged from what she has suffered at
the hands of these scoundrels. She did not even recognize her
own sister."

"Good God! This passes all bearing!" Frederick exploded into
violent oaths, then got himself in hand. "Go on, go on. Where
is she?"

"I suspect, sire, that Grimm is bringing her to Berlin, with
the intention of obtaining her inheritance from the bankers
involved. I am taking proper measures, in such an event.
Knowing that Your Majesty will protect this unfortunate girl—"

"She shall become a ward of the crown," Frederick exclaimed
with energy. "But what about proofs? I want proofs of all this
to lay before the French ambassador. I want confessions from

these scoundrels. This man Grimm must be found, taken alive, and put to the question!"

"That, sire, is my earnest and immediate endeavor. Meantime, his chief assistant is outside."

THE KING started. "Here? His chief assistant?"

"Yes, sire; an Englishman by birth, a man of great ability, who has been in the French service until lately." Count Otto delicately helped himself to snuff. "An honest fellow, whose conscience revolted at taking part in such villainy. It was he who provided us with the means of finding the poor girl. I've taken him into my employ, and—"

"Bring him here. Instantly."

Mortlake entered. He spoke very respectfully, with a perfect calmness which was most impressive. For two years an assistant to the French secret agent Luther Grimm, he had finally recoiled in horror, he said, at becoming involved in this hideous plot against a beautiful and innocent girl.

The aroused Frederick examined him severely and in detail. Few men, thus relating a sheer fabrication of lies, could have withstood the piercing questions, the razor-keen wit, the probing eyes, of Frederick; but Mortlake was no ordinary man. He displayed none of his actual animosity toward Luther Grimm, but having acted as a secret agent for years, he knew enough about his own business and that of Grimm to tell a most convincing story. Also, he himself was practically unknown, while Grimm's *coups* within the past few years had come to general notice.

AT LENGTH the King swung around to Osbrock.

"I want this man kept at hand. His sworn statements must be prepared in due form."

"Certainly, sire. They'll be upheld by other witnesses upon their arrival here. Meantime, Mortlake will be of the utmost service in apprehending this man Grimm, should he reach Berlin, and in the rescue of the young lady."

At these words, the one flaming eye of Mortlake flashed to Count Otto with an unspoken question. It was his first intimation that Grimm might be coming here, and that the tissue of falsehoods he had just uttered in regard to the American might have to stand against unpleasant refutation.

"Very well; the affair is in your hands." Frederick suddenly turned upon Mortlake. "Get out!" he barked at the top of his voice. "Out of here! I want to speak with Count von Osbrock in private."

Mortlake bowed and retired. When the door had closed behind him, Frederick fastened his keen and penetrating gaze on the Count.

"Now, Otto, suppose we talk business," he said briskly. "You're the most typical specimen I know of this accursed human race; but in your way, you're valuable. I rather suspect that you engineered the alliance I'm offered with England—the substantial subsidy that will be paid me if I follow my chivalric impulses and make war on France."

The words came with a sneer. The King went on rapidly:

"Without this Courland money, I'll enter no such alliance. To obtain the cash, the young lady must appear before the bankers Arnheim and Pfalzar, here in Berlin, make satisfactory proof of her identity, and sign the releases and receipts. Once she's here, we'll see that she does it; but I don't want anyone else to see that she does it. Do you comprehend?"

An almost imperceptible dew of perspiration stood on Count Otto's brow.

"Perfectly, sire. My men are now watching those two bankers."

"Don't let them leave the city…. Now, the Bavarian situation: I can't very well make war on Austria and France at the same time. If I receive satisfactory proofs that France has really backed this dastardly scheme against Marie of Courland, well and good."

"Your Majesty shall receive them."

"If I don't, then I shall stand up for the poor down-trodden people of Bavaria and become their champion against Austrian rapacity." Another sneer. "So, Otto, if you're interested in seeing the English alliance go through—get to work, produce a confession from this man Grimm, produce your sister-in-law, and get that money. That's all. Clear out!"

Count von Osbrock obeyed, not without relief.

Upon returning to the courtyard where his carriage waited, he found Mortlake also waiting. The one-eyed man followed him to the carriage and got in after him. Neither spoke until the vehicle was on its way; then Mortlake leaned forward.

"So Grimm is coming here, eh? What's happened?"

"Everything," said Count Otto, sniffing at his lace handkerchief. "That man has the devil's own luck! We've been unable to find Marie of Courland. I'm sure Grimm is bringing her here to get the money. Now, for your information, I'll tell you all that has taken place—"

He proceeded to do so.

Mortlake, whose massive features were marked by a certain pallor at all times, said not a word more. He listened without comment to all that Count Otto related; his silence was ominous, pregnant with suppressed and bursting emotions.

OSBROCK HAD two residences here in Berlin, one in the city, the other in the suburbs. It was to his town house the carriage now proceeded; by the time they reached it, Mortlake had the whole story of the events in the Rhineland. That is to say, the story as Count Otto chose to relate it.

The two men left the carriage, entered the house, and went to a library dark with books and gloomy with stiff old portraits. Once in this room, Mortlake became a different person. His dominant energy, his force of character, seemed to fill the whole place; the expression that crept into his face was terrible. Count Otto regarded him uneasily.

"So you killed St. Denis, eh?" These were Mortlake's first words. "Good! I only wish I'd done it. Now, I know this Luther

Grimm; I know what he'll do and how he'll do it. We must act together."

Count Otto thumbed his yellow mustache. "Precisely," he said, and waited. The one flaming eye of Mortlake dwelt upon him intently.

"This woman he's bringing, this Marie of Courland: what do you want done with her? We must have the truth now, at all costs. I must know exactly what end you desire to reach, before we take action."

Count Otto fingered his snuffbox. He had lied heavily to Frederick, which was no light matter. This man Mortlake must make good the lie.

"I don't want her harmed, if that's what you mean," he said nervously. "She must not be injured; but she must be apprehended. Lodge a charge of insanity against her and have her locked up; that's all. The King will deal with her himself; both he and I stand to profit by the matter."

"And you said that I'd profit also if we succeeded in this business," Mortlake said calmly. "To what extent?"

"Half a million francs."

"You take her inheritance; I take a crumb, eh? But it's no crumb to me. For that sum," Mortlake went on with a cold intensity, "I'd guarantee to catch King Frederick or the devil himself! Count it done, if I must go through hell to do it!"

"Uninjured, remember!"

Once again that baleful smile of disdain twisted the lips of Mortlake.

"Have no fear. Probably I know more about the family of Courland than you do, even if you married into it."

Once again uneasiness flitted into the pale blue eyes of Count Otto. Alone with this man, he was far from being the master; and he was unhappily aware of the fact. At this instant, however, a servant knocked and entered.

"Highness! There's a man outside, a courier. He says you know him. His name is Goetz, and—"

"Goetz! Flora's postilion." Count Otto straightened up. "Show him in, quickly!"

A MAN, dust-covered, hollow-eyed, staggering for want of rest and sleep, stumbled into the room.

"Well? What is it? Where is the Countess?" Count Otto demanded.

"In Dortstadt, Highness. She—she sent this."

Count Otto, his eyes very bright and sparkling, seized the sealed paper that the courier extended.

"Good. You may leave; they'll give you food and a place to sleep."

The man staggered out. Count Otto tore open the letter. An expression of savage joy came into his features. He thrust the missive at Mortlake.

"You read French? Here! I was right, I was right!"

The note was a hasty scrawl:

> *Otto: I am ill; I must come on slowly. Marie was here, disguised as a man. Grimm was with her. They have gone on to Berlin, with a private carriage. Jacques, the old servant of my father, is with them.*
>
> *Adieu.*
>
> *—Flora.*

Mortlake lifted an exultant face.

"I've not seen this girl Marie for some years. You have a picture of her?"

"You've seen my wife? The features are almost identical."

"No. I've not seen your wife for some years either." Mortlake smiled thinly. "My dealings have been with you, not with your wife."

"True. Well, I have a miniature here; I'll give it to you presently."

"Then that's settled." Mortlake drew a deep breath. "My business, however, now lies with Luther Grimm. He's coming here. Hm! You said he was disguised as an obscure notary? Then look out for him in the guise of a fine gentleman, of a prince! I tell you, I know that man's methods of work! He has the audacity of the devil. And I know his face, too; he can't fool me."

Count Otto nodded. "Very well. What now?"

"Work!" A flash of savage energy passed through the one eye, the entire face, of Mortlake. "That courier came from Dortstadt in Saxony, he said? Get maps, maps! I want to see the main highways leading to Berlin."

Count Otto had maps at hand, and spread them out over the big library table. While Mortlake pored over them, Count Otto frowned slightly over his own thoughts, and presently voiced them.

"This Grimm must die before he can do any talking, before he reaches here. Mortlake, be prepared to swear to all you told the King; I'll have other witnesses to back you up in each detail. As to the girl—"

"She is not insane, as you said," Mortlake interrupted.

"Leave that to me. My wife is skillful with drugs; a certain powder will give her all the appearance of insanity for some days at a time. We used it once before, when we carried her off to Cologne. We can use it now, if King Frederick sees her. Yes, all that can be handled very neatly—but only if this Luther Grimm dies!"

"You may confide his fate to me," said Mortlake calmly, but with an intensity of passion in his voice. "You see this blind eye? The tip of a rapier did it, in London. The rapier was in the hand of Luther Grimm. When he might have killed me, he merely blinded one eye, and went his way."

"He made a great mistake," said Count Otto thoughtfully.

"He did." Mortlake went on in his phlegmatic way: "He is dangerous. You might kill St. Denis, but you could not kill him. He has something few men possess—the power of killing the man who faces him with a sword. This is not a question of fence,

Here was no polished gentleman up to every
trick of fence, but a swordsman who was after
results only.... Luther Grimm found himself
fighting for his life as never before.

of skill, of finesse or luck. It's something inside him. If you ran
this man Grimm through the heart, he would still kill you."

"I understand what you mean, being something of a swordsman myself," Count Otto said softly. "You seem to admire him."

"I hate him with all my soul," was the calm reply. "But I don't
underestimate him. And I don't intend to meet him sword in
hand, either. Now look at the map. I see two possible routes
here from Dortstadt, two places where he might be caught. We
should do this as distant as possible from Berlin. He may come
here direct by way of Kyritz, or around through Wittenberg.
Am I correct?"

Count Otto nodded, alertly.

"Yes. One of us must go to Kyritz, the other to Wittenberg."

"And neither of us must go alone."

"Right." Count Otto dabbed at his mustache. "Shall we
say—three men with each of us? Not police, but officers,

swordsmen. We've no lack of splendid talent here in the King's service, soldiers of fortune, gentlemen who ask no questions. Hm! I'll give you the best of them, Mortlake, since you're no swordsman.

"Let us say, Chevalier de Castine; he outpointed me with foils a few weeks ago, and has few equals with the steel. Seingalt, that rascal of a Dane who has killed half a dozen men in duels— the same deadly quality you mentioned, Mortlake. And for the third, to be certain, let's say that rakehelly Hungarian captain of hussars, Baron Horvath. He's superb with the saber, actually superb. Suppose you take these three; they'll each have a soldier as lackey, giving you six men. Enough? I'll pick others to ride with me."

"Very well." The one flaming eye of Mortlake danced with an infernal satisfaction. "But these men are officers. They'll not take orders from me."

"They'll take my orders, and my money; never fear, they're not fine gentlemen to be overparticular." And a thin smile twisted Count Otto's little yellow mustache. "I must obtain leave for them, pay them, and send them here to ride with you. I have a dozen horses here, more in the stables of the house outside town; take your pick. In an hour, your three men will be here, with their servants."

Mortlake nodded. "Still one thing more: the likeness of this lady who's worth half a million francs to me."

Count Otto went to a desk, opened it, and brought to light a miniature set in a frame of gold and brilliants.

"Here; the sisters are almost exactly similar. But be careful! Her beauty, her youth, her sex, might tempt you!"

"Nothing can tempt me, where it's a question of half a million francs," Mortlake rejoined calmly, and handed back the miniature. "I'll know her again, disguised or not; she has changed quite a little since I last saw her. Now for the final detail: Knowing Grimm as I do, I fancy that he'll circle around and come by way of Wittenberg. He may not, of course. Which of us goes where?"

Count Otto shrugged lightly.

"As you like; it's indifferent to me. I'll go to Kyritz, you to Wittenberg. But waste no time getting there!"

"I'll waste neither time nor words, on this errand," Mortlake said grimly.

CHAPTER IX

U PON AN early afternoon Luther Grimm saw the old gates of Wittenberg opening ahead. A good day's run was already behind them, and Berlin was a scant sixty miles farther. All promised well.

These days of travel, of rest, of good food and better companionship, had worked a startling change in Grimm. The old fire had come back into his eyes. His hurts bothered him no more, and were forgotten; indeed, a debonair and reckless gayety unusual to him had crept into his manner.

The girl opened the flap behind the driver's back, and spoke with Jacques.

"Don't go to the post tavern. Instead, drive on through town and go to the Roten Hahn. It's an old inn on the farther side of town, and much safer for us. We'll leave M. Grimm there, and you can bring me back into town."

They rattled through the ancient, narrow streets of the old university city. Before reaching the Elbe, their road swung northward, on outside town again, and the horses came to a halt in the court of a massive old tavern.

"If I'm to return here as a woman, I'd better not appear as a man now." And Marie, laughing, refused to follow Grimm from the carriage. "I'll get everything I need, go to a hairdresser's, and the transformation will be complete. I'll need a couple of hours at least. We'd better leave the luggage in the carriage until I return. You can see about the rooms. You have money?"

"Plenty. Good luck!" and Grimm waved his hand blithely as the carriage started off, heading back to town. He turned to the landlord and the disappointed grooms. "Later, my friends, later! We'll want two private rooms, also quarters for our driver, but meantime there's no haste. I'll have something to eat, and a bottle of your best wine."

THE DAY was chill, lowering with fog and low clouds, threatening rain. A good day to be off the roads, reflected Grimm.

With a sigh of relaxation, he settled down at a corner table in the main room of the tavern, and loosened his sword-belt. The mammoth fireplace with its spits and chains held a fire for cooking, but the huge tiled porcelain stove was fireless at this season.

Grimm looked about the main room of the ancient tavern with quick interest. It was a vast place, overhung by blackened oak beams of enormous size. The walls were hung about with weapons of all kinds, relics of the wars that had burst over Prussia during these past hundred years.

The landlord, bringing bread and cold meat and wine, shook his head at Grimm's question. The place was two hundred years old and more, he said.

"But it's not what it was, Excellency. When the Austrians were here, eighteen years ago, they left everything bare as a bone. You see those sabers hanging behind the stove? They came from some of the Hungarian cavalry who were killed just outside here…. Ah! We have more customers. Your Highness has brought us luck today."

Horses had clattered into the inn yard. Luther Grimm paid no heed, for he was curiously examining the armor close at hand. His table was close to a short flight of six stairs which ascended to a raised floor—a room for banqueting parties, no doubt. These steps were flanked by two ancient suits of massive armor set upon posts, each one holding in its steel gauntlets a weapon. One held an immense two-handed Swiss sword; the other, rather incongruously, held a Hungarian saber.

Suddenly Luther Grimm started up, listening. A voice reached him faintly from the courtyard. He frowned, then rose and made his way across to a window that opened on the inn yard.

"Nonsense, of course," he muttered. "And yet I'd know that calm, penetrating voice of Mortlake's anywhere!"

He stood at the window. A man, hatted and cloaked, had just turned his horse and was riding away; he was out of the courtyard and gone. The others in the party held the questing gaze of Grimm. Three officers, he saw, in gay uniforms, and as many lackeys, soldier-servants. The man who had just departed must have been one of the party.

Nothing here, reflected Luther Grimm, to remind him of Mortlake. He had fancied a resemblance in one of the voices— sheer imagination! The three officers were grouped about the landlord, who looked frightened and was arguing with them: a Frenchman, a brawny Norman with red mustache and swaggering air; another, a thin and impassive-looking man, with a queer, indefinable suggestion of a death's head in his sunken features; the third was slim, dark, laughing, a man all fire and impulse, in a hussar officer's uniform, with saber dangling against his knee. Grimm looked again at the first, the brawny Norman, and then went back to his seat, frowning.

"Hm! Three wild blades there—and certainly I know that fellow with the red mustache!" He probed at memory; then his face cleared. "Castine; that's the name. Chevalier de Castine. He was turned out of the army three years ago for some disgraceful affair. I remember, yes; he was a fencer of great skill. So now he's in the Prussian service, like half the adventurers in Europe! Well, I wish Frederick joy of him."

INTO THE big tavern room came the three officers, swaggering and talking loudly. The thin, impassive man with face like a skull, was speaking in German.

"So our friend will be back, will he? I tell you, I don't like that fellow. I don't like Englishmen."

"Well, spend your money and don't vent your spleen on the man who provides it," exclaimed the Chevalier, twisting his red mustache and glancing about. "Here, let's have a table and be comfortable. You say you know this place, Baron Horvath. Any decent wine here?"

"The best in the world, my friends!" the Hungarian cried gayly. He turned to the landlord, who had followed them in. "Fetch some of that Tokay, a dozen bottles, and then clear out. Don't bother us unless we call for you. Give our men food and wine, feed the horses, and leave us alone."

The three settled themselves at a table, and the landlord brought in bottles of wine, for which he was promptly paid.

GRIMM REGARDED them in some astonishment and more amusement. Now and again their glances touched on him but showed no interest. A queer trio, he thought; the big Norman, ruffling it with many an oath; the thin man, whom they called Seingalt, with something about him that was cold and deadly; and the merry, impetuous Hungarian, who was a handsome fellow.

So the man who had left them and ridden away was an Englishman! Grimm felt an uneasy twinge. That English voice—certainly it had made him think of Mortlake. However, his imagination must have jumped at conclusions there.

He went on with his meal. A soldier came in, approached the three officers, saluted Castine and spoke with him. One of the three strikers or lackeys. Another salute and he departed. The three officers laughed and fell into low talk among themselves; they appeared to be settling some argument. Grimm kept a casual but interested eye on them.

At length Baron Horvath, the Hungarian, laughed gayly and his voice lifted.

"Bah! I don't care what the fellow told us. I don't care how famous a swordsman our man may be. I do know Castine's the best blade in the Army—even better than you, Seingalt. You Danes are too stiff in the wrist. Oh, I admit you may kill your man more quickly, but you'd lose on points. Fencing and killing aren't the same thing, by a long shot! I'll bet you twenty rix-dollars that Castine finishes the business inside five minutes."

"Done with you," said the gloomy Dane. "It's a bet—remember it!"

Grimm understood now. These officer's had ridden from Berlin, no doubt, to meet with some one else and settle a dispute of honor; it was a question of a duel. And here in this very room, perhaps, since they had all been so insistent on being left alone.

That their insistence on this point was no mere passing fancy, presently was made clear when the landlord came back into the big room. With him was a serving-wench, bringing fowl to set on the spits at the hearth.

The three officers erupted in a storm of angry oaths. Horvath, with a laugh, leaped up and went to the girl, swept his arm around her, and kissed her heartily. The wench struggled against him, caught up a goose in one hand, and swinging it by the neck, began to lambaste him over the head.

A scream of protest broke from the landlord, but now Seingalt and Castine were upon him, angrily sending him out with a kick and a volley of curses. He fled. The Hungarian was roaring with laughter and dodging the blows of the girl. Seingalt tried to interfere, caught the naked goose across the face full force, and went staggering. Castine, however, pinioned the arms of the wench and rushed her out of the room, while Baron Horvath doubled up against the wall with laughter, as the angry and chagrined Seingalt picked himself up.

Luther Grimm, looking on, broke into laughter himself at the scene. The three officers, returning to their table, caught sight of his expression and stopped short. All three stared at him. In their faces he read an ominous concentration.

"Your pardon, gentlemen, your pardon," he exclaimed. "Upon my word, I was laughing with you, not at you!"

"It's a pity to kill you,
but that's my business,"
said Horvath. "Pick up
your blade, my friend."
"Wait!" Grimm gasped.
"If it's money you're
after, I can pay you—"

The Chevalier made a gesture to his companions.

"To you, the doors," he said briefly. "To me, the man."

THEN, SWINGING around, he strode toward Grimm. The other two men sauntered off: the Dane to the kitchen doorway, the Hungarian to that opening on the courtyard. And suddenly Luther Grimm wakened to approaching trouble. He recalled the voice of the Englishman.

"I believe you may find better amusement," said the Chevalier ominously, halting and eying him straitly. "Are you not Monsieur Luther Grimm, the gentleman whose skill with the rapier has astonished Paris?"

They knew him—they knew him! In a flash, Grimm realized the truth.

"No," he said coolly. His harsh features tensed, gave darker significance to his whimsical response. "No; it has astonished nobody, I assure you. The dead, monsieur, are never astonished."

Castine twirled his mustache and puffed out his cheeks.

"Ha! Loud words, my friend, loud words! You displease me. Perhaps you are not aware with whom you deal?"

Grimm had already made up his mind, determined his course. These three men were here to kill him. If they attacked him all at once, he was lost. Since they had already arranged to take him in turn, he must hold them to that arrangement—and do what he could. But at the thought of Marie back in the town, of that Englishman who had ridden away, he went cold. Mortlake, of course.

"I'm entirely aware of it," he broke in coldly. "The reputation of the Chevalier de Castine is very well known, and bears out his present occupation as a hired assassin."

CASTINE FLUSHED and clapped hand to sword-hilt.

"You insult me, you rascal?"

"If that were possible," said Grimm coolly. "I sha'n't ask who paid you for this job; I can guess the answer. But before you put me out of my unhappy life, pray tell me one thing: The

Englishman who was with you when you arrived—did he have only one eye?"

"Yes," said Castine, with a savage scowl.

That settled it. Grimm's manner changed. An icy calm settled in his gaze, as it flicked from Castine to the other two.

"I see." His voice whipped out scornfully. "And you left your pistols with your horses, your men outside? Why, gentlemen, I'm surprised at such chivalry! You came here to kill me—surely you don't expect to give me a chance for life?"

The Hungarian laughed out, from the door he guarded.

"The very fact that we're here removes all chances, *mon ami!*"

"You think well of yourselves, eh?"

"Enough talk; we're not assassins," exclaimed the Chevalier angrily—the more so because they were, in effect, assassins, and he knew it well. "You have the appearance of a gentleman. Draw, then! I've no desire to kill an unarmed man."

"Thank you, monsieur," said Grimm.

He bared his rapier; a very fair weapon, though nothing of which to boast. He unbuckled the belt, and with it removed his coat, and gave the Norman a thin smile.

"Let me repay your chivalry," he said with light mockery. "This is not a duel, it seems, but a bit of unpleasant work to be got over with as soon as possible. Yet it would be distinctly unfair, did you meet me while encumbered by your coat. And it might even spoil the invention of my friend Raffini."

Castine, scowling suspiciously, stepped back and began to remove his uniform coat, watching Grimm narrowly for fear of some trick.

"Who the devil is your friend Raffini?" he demanded.

Luther Grimm laughed a little, as he tried the balance of his rapier.

"Oh, he's an Italian who came to Paris last year. He invented a most pleasing little touch, a new sort of parade in *prime;* I shall be delighted to show it to you, my dear Chevalier, although it will cause your friend Baron Horvath to lose his wager, by a good three minutes."

"Crow, cockerel, crow!" The Norman caught up his sword and strode forward. "Ready? *En garde*—"

The two men saluted, touched blades—and the two slivers of steel hung in air.

Grimm was frightfully aware of the truth: Mortlake had brought these men here, had set them on him, then had departed hastily. It all argued the one frightful certainty, that the Englishman would seize Marie, and then return here.

Assured of this, Luther Grimm settled implacably to work. A slight, bitter smile twisted his lips. The Chevalier attacked with a burst of fury, but Grimm's rapier hung almost motionless in a seeming miracle of defense.

"Careful!" he said lightly. "I sha'n't waste more than the one thrust—remember, the parade in *prime!* It's really a charming novelty. A pity that you can't carry away the memory of it, but that will be impossible. The fact that you don't know Raffini renders the outcome certain."

Sweat was starting on the Norman's broad features, as he found himself unable to pierce that defense. Fury grew upon him. He began to lose his head. With a rush, he flew in to a savage attack. A gasp of exultation broke from him as an opening appeared, as Grimm's arm and steel lifted high; he sent in a vicious thrust, straight and true, for the heart—

The thrust ended in air. Grimm's point darted down, darted in, and was gone again. The American leaped backward and stood panting.

"Twenty rix-dollars lost, Baron Horvath!" he exclaimed in grim jest. "Pay up, pay up!"

The Chevalier seemed paralyzed. A smear of scarlet suddenly gushed from his throat and lips, spreading over his shirt. He dropped his sword, clapped both hands to his throat, took a step backward and another step; his knees gave way and he pitched down in a heap.

"No need to examine him. That stroke never fails," said Luther Grimm harshly.

The Dane sprang forward, stooped above the fallen Castine, then rose. Ferocity was in his sunken features, as he stripped off cross-belts and uniform coat.

"Try it on me, if you like," he snarled.

Grimm measured him briefly, stood relaxed, controlling his heaving breath, hoping for time here. Baron Horvath, his eyes alight, came forward.

"No need to guard the doors," he said. "This man isn't running from us. You win the wager, Seingalt—payment later, if you live! Evidently that Englishman told us the truth. This fellow knows how to use a sword."

Luther Grimm waited. In the face, in the manner of this Dane, he perceived the killer. Here was no polished gentleman up to every trick of fence, but a more dangerous swordsman, one born and not made, who was after results only. No repeating that thrust with this man, who had just seen it work and was now prepared for it.

"You gentlemen are still intent on earning your pay?" said Grimm acidly.

Seingalt, for response, came striding at him with intent eyes. Small head, long agile arms, a wrist like steel. There was no salute. The Dane came straight in with a swiftly vicious lunge of his blade, and steel clashed and slithered.

Abruptly, Luther Grimm found himself fighting for his life as never before.

Silent, venomous, unwinking eyes like those of a rattle-snake—the man was death personified. His very air was calculated to freeze an opponent into panic. Grimm stood like a wall to the attack, then leaped backward as Seingalt broke into motion. The two moved about swiftly, in a rippling flow of action, springing in and out, steel darting; the very blades seemed alive and fluid.

MINUTES PASSED. Neither man had an advantage. Grimm was wholly on the defensive; he evaded trick after trick, parried almost blindly. This was fighting, not mere fence. Suddenly Seingalt disengaged, leaped backward, threw his sword from one hand to the other and drove in again—rapier in his left hand, now.

Almost did the trick catch Grimm napping. He felt a slight prick, heard a cry from the Hungarian, saw the blaze in Seingalt's eyes as the touch of red appeared on his shirt, and desperately called up every energy. A mere prick, but an inch more would have been death.

The Dane pressed in savagely, but now Grimm was bringing his brains into play. He attacked in turn, engaging Seingalt on the outside of the arm, trying to get under the arm with a *glissade,* sweeping repeatedly into a counter in *carte.* With any other man, this would have meant disarming him, but the Dane only laughed and evaded. Again Grimm found himself on the defensive. Now it was Seingalt who was trying to disarm him, and he bent every effort to meet the attack. The two men were steaming, eyes straining, rapiers quivering.

THE DANE began to give. Grimm's heart leaped as he met the look of fear in those glittering eyes. He pressed in with a dazzling display of feints and *ripostes.* In the midst, he stepped in the pool of blood that had come from the body of Castine. His foot slipped. He lost balance.

Seingalt's blade curled about his, tore it from his hand, and sent it hurtling across the room. Grimm plunged down. He had one flashing glimpse of the Dane poised, above him, darting in the finishing stroke.

Not for nothing had Luther Grimm, along the Pennsylvania frontier, risked his neck in wrestling matches with Daniel Morgan and many another backwoods champion. In the very act of falling, he twisted about. As he struck the floor and gained purchase, his foot flew out and struck the Dane's ankle. That vicious death-lunge was spoiled. Grimm rolled aside. His hand found the fallen rapier of the Norman, and he was up like a cat, up and almost breast to breast with Seingalt.

His left hand flew up and struck the Dane full in the face. As the cursing Seingalt staggered back, Grimm straightened; the rapier in his hand ran the man through the body. Then he stumbled away, panting, dabbing the sweat out of his eyes, until he came against one of those posts bearing armored figures. He clung to it, exhausted.

There was a crash. Grimm's eyes cleared, to see Seingalt fallen, and the Hungarian leaning over him.

"Ha! That saves me paying the wager." Baron Horvath straightened up, an excited laugh on his lips, his eyes shining. He flung off his *pelisse* and *sabretache* and belt; the curved saber was in his hand, its loop about his wrist.

His lungs afire, his nerves quivering with exhaustion, Grimm knew himself unable to meet any attack from this man. The rapier in his hand was useless against that slashing weapon, He let it fall, and it clanked to the floor. Horvath halted.

"Come, come! Pick it up. It's a pity to kill you, but that's my business. The money goes to me, instead of being split among three, and so much the better. However, pick up your blade, my friend."

Aching muscles, weariness, sword-arm like lead—Grimm stirred a little. Metal clinked under his hand. He was clinging to the armored figure which held the saber. His brain wakened; time, a moment of time, anything for time!

"Wait!" he gasped. "If—if it's money you're after—I can pay you—"

"No, no, it's a matter of honor, my dear fellow!" The Hungarian laughed wildly. "Besides, see what you've done to my comrades!"

"At least," said Grimm, "two of you have helped pay for my friend St. Denis."

"I never heard of him, but you're about to pay for these two gentlemen." And the Baron swished his saber lightly. "That rascally Englishman will soon be back here with your lady—he promised to bring her—and I can't disappoint him."

Mortlake, back here with Marie! A burst of energy surged through Luther Grimm at the thought. The spell that bound him was broken. Strength flooded into his hand, as he plucked at the saber held between the fingers of the steel gauntlet. It came away in his hand, and he sprang on guard.

"Hello!" A laugh broke from the lips of Horvath. "Upon my word, one could almost admire such a fellow! Ready?"

"Almost." Grimm's pounding heart was lessening its strokes. "Did you ever hear of the Polish noble in Vienna—Pan Lichestski?"

Horvath's eyes widened.

"Lichestski? Who hasn't heard of that man?" he exclaimed. "Why, they say he's a magician! The greatest master of the saber in the world, that fellow. What put him into your head?"

LUTHER GRIMM, controlling his sobbing breath, smiled thinly. Every instant of time meant much now.

"He told me, once, that there's one thing even the greatest master of the saber forgets."

"And what is that?" demanded Baron Horvath curiously.

"Ah! He also told me it was something never to be told—only shown."

"You knew him?"

"I was his pupil for six months."

"Then," said the Baron, as he moved forward, "I certainly was a fool to let you get your breath. At you!"

And with a swinging rush, a stamp of feet, a whistle of the blade in his hand, he was attacking like a whirlwind.

GRIMM STOOD between those two figures of ancient armor and met the attack unmoving. Frantic desperation held him cool, composed; from the first moment, he realized that if he tried any attack, he was lost. Here was a master of the weapon, a man whose agility and skill far outshone his own.

He stood like a rock. Horvath beat at him from every side; the clang of the steel reëchoed from the black rafters, as the blades clashed together. Almost too rapidly for eye to follow whirled that flaming steel—but Grimm's eye followed it; his own blade met the back-drawn slash each time. The curved steel above his head flashed ever in an arc that yielded not.

The Hungarian, white teeth showing in a snarl, slashed low for the knees, slashed in from one side or the other, always found that glinting wall of steel before him and could not break it. He feinted, deliberately left openings, gave Grimm repeated chances to whip in a lightning blow—and the American refused each offer.

None the less, it was a fresh man against a wearied man.

Sparks were dancing before Grimm's eyes. Every effort was toilsome, now; his arm was giving out. Only blind desperation, a stubborn determination, held him to the task, forced him to await the time for the one thing he could do.

The Hungarian was winning, and knew it. Exultation filled his sweating visage; he pressed his attack with a superhuman energy, a deadly precision. Obviously the American was weakening fast, meeting each slash, each cut, more slowly.

Horvath leaped back, dashed sweat from his eyes, peered at Grimm.

"So there's one thing every *beau sabreur* forgets, eh?" he panted. "Well, you'll never get a chance to tell me now."

And he was in again with a terrific cut that Grimm barely managed to parry. He meant to finish the business now; he launched a dazzling assault, blade whistling, his eyes flaming with fury.

"What is it, what is it?" he gasped, as he slashed in and in, until they were almost breast to breast. "Speak up! What is it—before I kill you?"

Grimm suddenly stepped backward, parried again, moved too fast for eye to catch.

"That—that the saber—has a point!" he croaked out, as his blade drove.

His hoarse croak was echoed by a frightful cry from the Hungarian. Grimm's point had plunged into his breast, and was out again.

Horvath caught his blade in both hands. Blood foamed on his lips; his eyes were distended and horrible. He flung himself forward; his saber whirled; he brought it down in a terrible slash. Grimm had ducked away. The blade struck the figure of ancient armor and sheared through both helmet and gorget.

Grimm, ducking low, was hit by the falling helmet. It caught him over the ear and sent him sprawling headlong, dazed and half stunned. With a frantic effort he tried to gain his feet, only to collapse on the steps, his lungs afire and his senses all aswim, helpless to move.

He was dimly aware of a low groan and a crashing thud as the Hungarian went down….

Presently Grimm's eyes cleared a little, and with an effort he lifted his hand to his head. The skin was not broken; he was unhurt. Baron Horvath, six feet away, was struggling to one elbow, was looking at him, was trying to speak.

"You—you were right," came the words on blood-bubbling lips, with ghastly grin. "One—one remembers that fact—too late."

The man's head fell, and jesting to the last, he smiled and died.

"Three for St. Denis," muttered Luther Grimm.

Still dazed, Grimm struggled to his feet and stood swaying, weak in every muscle. He staggered over to his own table and collapsed weakly in a chair. He reached for the wine in front of him but was unable to lift it to his lips. His body slumped in utter exhaustion; sparks were flying before his eyes.

From the courtyard came a roll of wheels, a clatter of hoofs. Mortlake!

Grimm made a convulsive effort. He started up, gasped out a low groan, and swayed limply forward across the table. He was done; he was utterly exhausted.

CHAPTER X

THE DARK little shops of Wittenberg were echoing now and again to strangely unwonted merriment and bursts of laughter. For here was a gayly cloaked gallant buying feminine attire, no less; in fact, the most intimate of feminine attire, while a dusty carriage waited in the street and the withered Jacques carried out the parcels.

At these close quarters Marie was not too successful with her manly pose, since her voice betrayed her, however huskily she lowered it. Now, however, this mattered very little.

The purchases were all made at last, and Jacques drove to a very handsome establishment on the Marktplatz, where the chief hairdresser of the town held forth. Marie went in with her parcels, while outside the carriage waited.

In this place Marie openly revealed her secret and prepared for her change back to woman's estate.

At last it was finished. Now she was clad as best became her, the Spanish cloak over her gown of stiff velvet, and a necklace about her throat. The black stain was washed out of cropped hair and arching brows. With a muslin catch-all spread above her garments, she sat in the hairdresser's chair to have her hair dried and curled—to conceal its short length.

A man came past the window as she sat there—a man whose hat was pulled so low over his face as to conceal his eyes, or rather eye; for he had but one. He glanced in as he passed, then peered sharply into the place.

Marie was too absorbed in her own metamorphosis to pay any attention to loiterers in the street. Her hair shimmered gold, once more, and it was built up with switches cleverly pinned fast.

When she had admired the work in the big mirror, she paid her bill and adjusted a fine lace shawl about her head. Humming a gay tune, she started out to the carriage. The head of old Jacques had sunk on his breast; he was asleep.

Smiling, Marie looked up at her old retainer. The hairdresser's clerk came out, bearing the only one of her purchases that was not upon her back at the moment. This was a large and handsome case of toilet accessories. Having the bag of gold still in the carriage, she had spent without stint.

Before a shop-front near by, the man with one eye was standing in talk with two other men, police by their somber uniforms; all three were watching her intently.

"Jacques!" she exclaimed, laughing. "Jacques! Wake up!"

He came awake with a start. In confusion, he began to clamber down to open the carriage door, but the grinning hairdresser's clerk forestalled him.

"Put the case inside," Marie ordered the clerk.

He did so, and held open the door. She got into the carriage. Eager, delighted with her new appearance, she settled down on the seat. Opening the case, she took out a mirror to view her features again.

Like the other fittings of the toilet case, the mirror was handsome. It was a large round glass set in a flat round frame and backing of chased copper; it was ornate, substantial and extremely heavy. Marie snatched a hasty glance at her hair, adjusted the clasp of the cloak at her throat, then looked up as Jacques came to the open window and addressed her.

"Where now, madam?"

"Oh! Back to the Roten Hahn, of course. Do I look all right?"

Jacques complimented her and started back to his seat. Then, glancing through the window-opening at her side, Marie glimpsed something that drew the color from her cheeks and widened her startled gaze.

The two police were moving toward the horses' heads; the other man was coming to the carriage window. That face, that one flaming eye—she had seen it in Treves, though the man had not remarked her there. She had remembered it in dreams; she had spoken of it to Luther Grimm. The face of the man who had ruined her family. The face of the Englishman Mortlake!

The heart failed in her. He was at the window, now, peering in at her, one hand on the door.

"A moment, madam, if you please," he said in French. At sight of her, shrinking, horrified, gripped by recognition and fear, he smiled grimly. "You remember me, do you? Well, you'll have no more use for this carriage, nor your friend Grimm either."

Mortlake! She knew they were both surprised and trapped. Almost unconscious of her action, with one convulsive spasm of sheer terror, she struck out at that deadly, flaming eye. A wild cry burst from her.

"Drive, Jacques, drive!"

Jacques, himself startled by the appearance of the two police,

Mortlake was at the window now. "You remember me?"... You'll have no more use for this carriage, nor your friend Grimm either."

curled his whip. The horses leaped. The police shouted in vain, then scrambled away.

Marie, unaware that Mortlake had disappeared from sight and was not following, sat frozen with terror, while the carriage went careering on its way.

But the Englishman was in no condition to do any following. When the girl lashed out with all her frantic strength, the chiseled edge of that mirror struck him full above the eyes; and he went down senseless as the carriage darted off.

Jacques drove like a madman through the narrow streets, until for the sake of safety Marie slowed him down. She opened the panel, with frantic words.

"The police—they must have been waiting for us. Mortlake himself! We can't spend the night here now. Reach the inn, get

Monsieur Grimm, and hasten on, anywhere! I don't know what to do. You run in and get him, at the inn."

The horses speeded again. They were past Luther's Oak, rolling out of town and on to the Roten Hahn. The bulk of it rose before them, and Jacques tooled the carriage into the courtyard. Other horses stood at one side; a tumult of frightened cries came to them. Grooms and landlord stood bawling and cursing.

Ignoring the lot of them, the old servitor was already scrambling down. He went at a run and vanished in the doorway; after a moment, Marie heard a faint cry, as though horror had seized upon him. She leaned forward, anxiously. The landlord and grooms, who appeared too terrified to approach her, made no reply to any question. Then Jacques reappeared. He was dragging Luther Grimm along with him, helping him into coat and wig and hat, shoving him toward the carriage.

CHAPTER XI

"WHAT'S HAPPENED?" called Marie. And Grimm, brought somewhat to himself by the ministrations of Jacques, straightened up. Her voice, the fresh air—yes, it was true. Marie was here, not Mortlake. A sudden laugh broke on his lips, as he came to the carriage.

"Get in, get in!" Marie swung open the door. "Mortlake's here. I saw him. He had police with him. He spoke of you, he was going to arrest me—oh, we must be off quickly!"

"I believe you!" Grimm swung up into the carriage. He waved his hand at the landlord and grooms, who had begun to bawl curses afresh; taking a gold-piece from his pocket, he flung it at them as Jacques started the horses. "Help yourselves to the dead gentlemen, lads! Their money's still good, if they're not!"

His eyes dancing, he fell back on the cushions. Marie stared at him.

"Dead gentlemen? What are you talking about? What are those men shouting about? Are you drunk?"

"Drunk, yes; drunk with beating the devil at his own game." With a deep breath, he relaxed. "Mortlake brought three men here to kill me. Well, they failed. What's that you said? You saw him?"

She shivered. "Yes, yes. He was at the door of the carriage— What are we to do?"

"That depends." Grimm inspected her curiously. "How the devil did you get away from him? What happened?"

"I—I hardly know," she faltered. "He was there, speaking to me; his one eye was like fire. He mentioned you. I knew him; I was terrified—"

Grimm patted her hand. "There, there, take it easy! I can't imagine how he failed to nip you. Police, you say?"

"Two of them." The toilet case was at her feet, still open. The mirror lay beside her. She pointed to it. "I was holding this. I struck at him—the way you strike out at something horrible in the darkness—oh, I was beside myself!"

She looked at her hand as though in horror, then at the mirror. Luther Grimm followed her gaze. He saw the smudge of nearly dried blood on the metal, and whistled softly as he picked it up.

"You hit him with the edge of this?" He swung the mirror and nodded. "A deadly thing, upon my soul! I with the saber, you with the mirror—ha! We've done well, you and I. But I hope you didn't kill him. I want that pleasure myself." He put down the mirror and looked back through the little rear window of the carriage.

"No pursuit," he said coolly. "So far, at least. Devil take me, comrade, if you're not one in a thousand! Let's see; Mortlake must have been watching in the town, perhaps at the gates, for our arrival. He followed us to the inn, left his friends there to kill me, went back himself to nab you—hm! I think all's safe ahead. When you came, I thought it Mortlake coming back to

finish me. I'd got a clip over the head that left me dazed—bah! Forget it all. Comrade, you've been my good angel throughout. By God, I've beaten them at their own game, and I'll do it again! We'll look ahead and not back, eh?"

"Never back, always ahead," she repeated, a glow in her face. And Grimm smiled again as he met her eyes.

Sunset and darkness drew down. They came to a village, made a hasty stop at the little tavern, and were on again with directions, food and wine. An hour later Jacques pulled up the horses and they dined by light of the carriage lanterns. It was only another hour to the next post tavern.

"We'll get fresh horses there," Grimm said to old Jacques. "We'll take on a postilion to drive and let you sleep inside. Keep going? By all means. Sixty miles to Berlin, and we must be there tomorrow night."

More than this he refused to say. As the horses raced on, he sat with biting eagerness in his spirit and plans taking shape in every detail. Once in Berlin, he would no longer be on the defensive. There, the game would be in his hands to play, the attack would be his to make.

At the next post-house they managed to secure fresh horses by dint of gold, with a postilion to take the reins. The worn-out Jacques fell asleep in the carriage. Opposite, Marie sat with Luther Grimm's arm bracing her against lurches of the vehicle; and they slept by snatches.

SIXTY MILES—FIVE post-stations and changes of horses—night wearing into day, day drawing on apace, with hasty pauses for refreshment but none for sleep. At the last halt, twelve miles out of Berlin, Grimm learned that a city-bound diligence would be along in a few moments—indeed, they had passed it on the road. He booked a place in it for himself, came back to the carriage as the horses were being changed, and abruptly bade the surprised Marie farewell.

"Safer now if we separate," he said. "Go straight to the Hôtel de Paris. Here's a note for Madame Rufin, who keeps the lodgings. She knows me; she can be trusted. As soon as you get there, go to bed and sleep for an hour. Then I'll come for you."

Astonishment, surprise, dismay, struggled in her eyes.

"You'll come for me? To go where?"

Grimm's eyes twinkled gayly.

"To get your inheritance—and money for the Continental Army! *Au revoir,* my dear, and good luck. You should be in Berlin by sunset or soon after."

He bent his lips to her fingers, gestured to Jacques, who had resumed the reins, and the carriage rolled away....

Grimm had time only for a hasty bite and a flagon of wine when the diligence came in. He took his place, and with swift changes of horses and shift of mail sacks, they were off. These last twelve miles passed swiftly. Sunset came, the daylight died; the pale stars were just appearing, when the journey was ended.

BERLIN! GRIMM alighted stiffly. Then as he strode unrecognized through the streets of Frederick's capital, the old keen thrill of the game surged across his pulse-beats, filled his veins, sent his spirit soaring. Luck was with him!

He came to the residence of the French ambassador, a spacious mansion set amid walled gardens. The gates were open, carriages thronged the drive, the house was glittering with lights. Grimm approached one of the lackeys at the gate.

"The Marquis d'Evrecourt is obviously at home?"

"He's entertaining at dinner, monsieur."

"Good. I've just arrived from Paris with important dispatches. Take me into the house by a side entrance, and summon your master."

"Have the kindness to follow me, monsieur."

Grimm was taken past the *porte-cochère* to a rear entrance and so into the house. With passing glimpses of a splendid assemblage, he was led to a large neat library, the *cabinet du travail* or working-office of the ambassador, and left to wait.

He was not long alone. The door opened. Evrecourt, in court attire, splendid with jeweled orders, came into the room and stopped short at sight of him.

"M. Grimm!" he exclaimed. "Upon my word, this is a happy surprise—I've been hoping you would come—"

Grimm smiled thinly. "And my business, I fear, threatens your evening's peace and quiet. Have you any word from Versailles for me? From the Count de Vergennes?"

"Yes, here in the desk. Be seated, I beg of you. While you're in the city, you must make your home with me."

Grimm made no response, but seated himself and got out his pipe and pouch.

From a drawer of his desk, Evrecourt took a letter addressed to him by the minister of France, together with a sealed enclosure bearing Grimm's name. He handed them to Grimm, who glanced first at the open letter. Vergennes had written briefly:

If M. Luther Grimm comes to you, I beg that you will hand him the enclosed, and place all your resources at his disposal.

With a heart-leap, Grimm tore open the sealed enclosure, glanced at it, then looked up as Evrecourt addressed him:

"My friend, I must warn you that I've heard some queer rumors. A word here, a word there. The King himself asked me yesterday whether you had not been implicated in some abduction. I assured him it was absurd. Apparently you've become well and unfavorably known of late. I don't understand it."

"No matter." Grimm filled his pipe, and glanced at the ormolu clock on the desk. "My dear Evrecourt, it's now seventhirty. In an hour's time, we decide the fate of Europe in this room. Do you know two bankers in the city named Arnheim and Pfalzar?"

"VERY WELL indeed," said the startled ambassador. "Arnheim is pro-France and has powerful business connections in Paris. He's dining here tonight, with his wife; they've not arrived yet."

Grimm's blue eyes flashed. "Good! And Pfalzar?"

"Not so good. A dour, hard old Prussian who hates everything French. I believe his interests lie rather in Russia and Hamburg. Both men are honest and of the highest standing. Their houses have no banking equals here."

"Very well. Send to Pfalzar and ask him to be here at eightthirty to the minute. Say that urgent business concerning a matter of two hundred million francs has arisen. At the same hour, bring Arnheim to this room. I'll be here, with a lady, to talk with these gentlemen. Can you arrange this?"

"Of course." Evrecourt eyed him keenly. "Two hundred millions? Then you certainly have discovered Aladdin's treasure cave! What else?"

"This." Luther Grimm lighted his pipe at a candle, and then spoke rapidly, curtly. The ambassador listened, but passed from uneasiness to consternation.

"My dear monsieur," he broke in at last, with a trace of formality, "what you ask is—well, it's preposterous! It's contrary to all diplomatic custom. As ambassador of France, I'd be outraging my position here. Further, do you know the King?"

"No, but I've met him. He's eccentric, of course—"

"Eccentric? He's a madman at times! He's capable of anything, anything! He has no regard whatever for conventions—"

"Neither have I."

"But he'd probably arrest me, throw me into prison."

Grimm saw that the stumblingblock he had feared was before him.

"Come, put an end to this nonsense," he said brusquely. His harsh, flinty features became cold as ice. "Are you aware that Frederick is about to become an ally of England and to declare war on France?"

"Eh?" Evrecourt stared blankly. "Of course not. Such a thing is out of the question. It's absurd. Why, he's preparing to make war on Austria!"

"Perhaps." Grimm puffed at his pipe, and his blue eyes chilled. "Friendship, my dear Marquis, must be forgotten in this emergency. Unless you do as I request, France faces ruin, as does my own country, as do my own people. Do you actually refuse to do as I request?"

"I must." Evrecourt spoke stiffly. "In my opinion, such an action would be an outrage to my position!"

"Let's trust that you'll change your mind very quickly." Luther Grimm removed the pipe from his mouth, and spoke slowly. "Unless you do, you'll leave this room under arrest; you'll leave Berlin inside an hour as a prisoner; and you'll end your journey in the Bastille. In your place, I'll appoint myself ambassador to the court of Berlin. Now, the choice is yours. Speak up—which is it to be?"

Evrecourt flushed deeply, then paled.

"M. Grimm, have—have you become a madman?"

By way of reply, Grimm extended the sealed letter he had

just ripped open. Evrecourt took it, glanced at it, and his eyes dilated. The epistle was curt:

> *DE PAR LE ROI: (In the King's name)*
> *Sieur Luther Grimm is given entire authority to act for France.*
> *Signed, LOUIS*
> *Countersigned, Vergennes.*

"This—but this is unheard-of! It is incredible—past belief!" stammered the ambassador.

Grimm laughed harshly, his eyes alight with gay flames.

"You just mentioned Aladdin; well, here's Aladdin's lamp, my dear Evrecourt. My friend Franklin knows me and knows his business, eh? Vergennes is utterly desperate. If Frederick becomes an ally of England, with a war chest all provided, France is lost, the war in America is hopeless. So, having some slight faith in my ability, they run the risk of sending me this authority. Now, I'm equally desperate, and my time's short. Let me have your decision, if you please."

The other made a gesture of futility.

"I'm in your hands; I'll do as you say. The responsibility is yours."

"Upon your word of honor, my dear Marquis?"

"Yes."

"Very well. This highly dangerous document has served its purpose, so I'll play fair with Vergennes." And leaning forward, Grimm held the note to the flame of a candle and watched it burn. "I'm off. I'll be back at eight-thirty, perhaps before then. I need two men to take my orders. You have agents at work here?"

"Yes, yes; I can reach them, that is. They're not in the house."

"Naturally not." Grimm rose, laughed, and clapped the confused man on the shoulder. "Come, Evrecourt! We're friends; we work together, for the same cause. I intend to see Frederick tomorrow. The police, I might add, would greatly appreciate getting their hands on me. Thus, I can't seek an interview in the regular way."

"See Frederick? You're utterly insane!" broke out Evrecourt chokingly. "If you do what you propose tonight, Frederick will have you shot on sight!"

Grimm chuckled. "That's my risk. Suggest something. How can I see him, or where, in some informal manner?"

The ambassador shrugged. "He stands on no formality, disregards all ceremony, makes appointments with his own hand. I'm to ride with him in the morning, to inspect his school for army cadets at Potsdam. We're to be there at nine. That is, I *was* to ride with him," added Evrecourt unhappily. "If you pull off this *coup* tonight, I'll probably be in prison tomorrow."

"Thanks; I'll keep your appointment at Potsdam, then. Come, cheer up! What I want you to do, this night, is no more than a threat. And it's for France, remember."

Evrecourt regarded him with lowering gaze, angry and resentful now.

"I'm not so sure of that, M. Grimm. I distrust your motives; I've heard queer rumors about you. You're no Frenchman. When I was in Paris in the spring, I understood you had left the service and had slipped away to America with young Lafayette in defiance of the royal orders. Now you show up here and prate about France, and order me to risk my position, to overturn the whole delicate foundation of diplomacy—"

Grimm lost patience.

"My dear Evrecourt, you're quite right," he broke out icily. "When you were in Paris, I was fighting the British in America. I've just come from there, racked with fever, with British bayonet-wounds across my body, my family and friends ragged and starving and desperate. A new nation is coming into life over there—and the damned diplomacy you talk about is trying to strangle it at birth. So I prate of France? Very well; have the truth: France be hanged! I'm not working for France—but you are! I'm working for my own people. I suppose your fine in-

stincts revolt at grubbing around in the dirt for the sake of
taking a woman's money away from her?"

"They do!" said Evrecourt with a certain hauteur, and Grimm's
eyes blazed.

"Mine don't. I'd grub in the gutters of hell in such a cause!
That woman made an offer. France has accepted it. I've accepted it, also. Why? To get her money? Let us say, rather—to
save the woman herself! France stands chivalric, noble, knight-
ly, to protect a poor woman against her enemies. France is the
champion of the helpless, against the rapacity of rogues and
thieves! That's the way France regards it. That's the way you
should regard it."

Evrecourt gave him a keen glance, then impulsively extended his hand.

As the Countess fled toward the gate, two figures were beside her in a flash. One low cry escaped her lips, unheard.

"I apologize, *mon ami;* also, allow me to say that I fear you are a terrible liar. Money, your friends, your country—bah! Perhaps that was your first aim. Now it is something else—it's a woman for whom you're fighting. Am I right?"

Grimm hesitated as their hands met. He shrugged, and relaxed his tension.

"Frankly—perhaps you are…. You mentioned two agents at hand. Who are they?"

Evrecourt named them, and Grimm beamed in delight; he knew them both.

"Splendid! Get word to them; have them report to me at the Hôtel de Paris in twenty minutes; kindly instruct them that I'm to be obeyed implicitly. And will you have the kindness to supply me with a carriage and driver at once?"

The ambassador assented. Grimm went on thoughtfully.

"Hm! Good thing we have two trusty men here. If I were in the place of Count von Osbrock, I'd certainly have a police spy keeping watch on the houses and offices of those two bankers."

"Osbrock?" Evrecourt's brows lifted slightly. "What has he to do with all this? Of course, the girl is his sister-in-law, but I don't see—"

Luther Grimm chuckled. "What you don't see, my dear Evrecourt, will remain painless. Better leave it that way."

So it came to pass, in the course of the evening, that the police spy who was keeping an eye on the residence of the banker Pfalzar was approached by two strangers. They engaged him in conversation, and without the least warning knocked him on the head.

As for the spy watching Arnheim's house, that was different. He was not bothered, since the banker was away from home for the evening.

IT WAS a curious group that gathered in the study of the French ambassador, a group eying one another with mingled emotions, and not pleasant ones either.

Luther Grimm was cool, alert, saying little. Marquis d'Evrecourt, to do him justice, played with a suave firmness the part to which he was forced. Marie, radiant but inwardly excited, watched the two bankers with smiling confidence as they examined her documents.

Of the two bankers, Arnheim was affable but nervous; Pfalzar was openly hostile. He was an iron-jawed man with shrewd and arrogant eyes, a totally different type from his more cultured fellow. He said what he thought.

"This demand, made in such a way and at such a time, is absurd," he declared with harsh finality. "I refuse to have anything to do with it."

"What?" Marie leaned forward in dismay. "Why, how can you say such a thing? You cannot refuse!"

Pfalzar bent his shaggy brows on her.

"How do we know you're the person to whom these documents refer? No!"

"I stand as guarantee," said Evrecourt with dignity.

"You?" Pfalzar shot him a savage look. "And what are you in this matter?"

"France."

Pfalzar grunted, disconcerted. Arnheim turned to him anxiously.

"The documents are in order, as you see. This young lady is guaranteed by France. Further, we both know her, though I have not seen her for some time. The proof is fully satisfactory, Pfalzar; and as an honest man you cannot deny it. Unless we meet the conditions of our trust, we cannot uphold our reputation as bankers—"

"Very well; granted!" Pfalzar snorted again. "But the demand must be made in the ordinary course of business, not in the dead of night and unexpectedly."

"It seems to me," put in Luther Grimm calmly, "that all the essential conditions have been met."

"That is true; yet the impossible is demanded of us." Arnheim turned to him with a helpless gesture. "We do not carry two hundred million francs in a waistcoat pocket. The books must be checked over by accountants; outstanding sums must be called in and verified; interest charges must be—"

Marie intervened with a smile.

"Gentlemen, you are right, quite right! However, here on the table are quills, ink and paper; to write bills-of-exchange requires only a few moments. Let me suggest a way out of your dilemma. Write bills on Paris for one hundred millions, payable to me or to my order. I'll then give you a receipt in full for the entire amount of my inheritance, leaving the amount in blank, on your word of honor that the balance due will be sent me in Paris within the next thirty days."

The bankers stared at her amazedly.

"What? Are you a fool?" exclaimed Pfalzar harshly. "You'd take our bare word?"

She flung him a quick bright smile.

"I follow the example of my father in trusting you, Herr Pfalzar. This will close the matter of your trust. It will leave you owing me approximately half the balance of my inheritance. As protection, if you desire to do so, give me a joint note to this effect, leaving the amount unspecified."

T H E   B A N K E R met the eagerly assenting gaze of his colleague. He hesitated; then his thin lips clamped shut for an instant.

"No," he broke out. "The money cannot go to you without our joint approval. I refuse to give mine here and now. Come to my office tomorrow, see to the affair in the usual way, and it's all very well. But I'll not be coërced into this unprecedented sort of thing. It's against all my principles."

To Luther Grimm, it was clear that this man was in the confidence either of Count Otto or of King Frederick. He glanced at Evrecourt and made a slight gesture. The ambassador rose and beckoned pleasantly to Pfalzar.

"Will you step to the window with me?" he said. The banker scowled, then rose and accompanied him. Grimm followed them both.

Pulling back the heavy curtain, Evrecourt pointed to the courtyard below, where a berlin was being fetched out and horses harnessed to it.

"In that carriage, my dear Pfalzar, is an extra large luggage-boot," said the ambassador confidentially. "A bound and gagged man might lie in it unseen, perfectly hidden, until the Prussian frontier was passed. He would, of course, be extremely uncomfortable. During his indefinite absence, his business would assuredly suffer very heavily—"

" W H A T   D O you imply?" growled Pfalzar, turning in fury. "Do you dare have the impudence to threaten me?"

"Alas, I would not venture. But this gentleman would." And with his most affable smile, Evrecourt indicated Grimm. "This Herr Grimm has no respect whatever for persons or laws. The carriage, yonder, takes him out of Berlin in ten minutes, my dear Pfalzar. And if you persist in your attitude—he takes you with him. Bound and gagged."

"What? You'd lend yourself, your position, to such an outrage?" Pfalzar gasped. "It's known to my family that I came here, at your request. If I don't return, the King will call you to answer in short order! Ambassador or no, he'd have you taken out and shot!"

"You may be right." And the marquis was unable to suppress a sigh. "However, that would not help you; you'd be far from here, and going farther."

"Precisely," put in Grimm. He met the glare of Pfalzar with his whimsical smile, but there was no smile in his blue eyes. "And while it would be a pity if M. d'Evrecourt were shot, how much greater a pity it were if Prussia were to become an ally of England!"

His gaze countered that of Pfalzar. He perceived instantly that the banker was aware of the entire intrigue; his shot went home and left the other speechless.

"You see what's at stake," he went on cheerfully. "Of course, if you insist on becoming a martyr to further the purposes of Otto von Osbrock, I'll oblige you. But I fear your reputation as a holder of trust-funds, as a financier, as a business man, will suffer irreparable damage."

Pfalzar was silent for a moment; the choleric hue of his empurpled features died into a slow pallor. Evrecourt let fall the curtain again. Their low words had not reached the others. Marie was talking with Arnheim.

"Very well, I must assent, it seems," snapped Pfalzar with a growling oath. "But I promise you His Majesty shall know of this outrage within the hour!"

"That," said Grimm, "is your privilege. Long before then, I'll be heading for the frontier with the young lady yonder; and we'll not be caught. If M. d'Evrecourt suffers, it will be in the service of his country."

Fuming, the banker rejoined his associate and gruffly gave his consent to the proposal of Marie.

"A moment of figuring, and we can arrange everything," said Arnheim. "To what address in Paris, mademoiselle, do we send the balance due you?"

Grimm struck in: "Why, if you please, in care of Dr. Benjamin Franklin, a gentleman who's quite well known there. But you may turn over the bills to M. d'Evrecourt, who'll forward them with his diplomatic dispatches."

The marquis was charmed to be of service, and said so. While the two bankers figured, Luther Grimm caught the eye of their host and drew him aside for a brief word in private.

"Have a courier ready to get off with that carriage the moment those bills-of-exchange are turned over, and Marie assigns them to M. de Vergennes. Get your man off on the instant, understand?"

Evrecourt's eyes opened. "But you said you were leaving—"

Grimm broke into a laugh. "While they're scouring the highways for me tomorrow, I'll be talking with Frederick. Quick! Get your messenger ready. And if you're in prison tomorrow, I'll either have you out before evening, or join you there."

Which was small consolation to the Marquis d'Evrecourt.

HALF AN hour passed before the papers were written out, signed and delivered. From odd remarks exchanged with the disgruntled Pfalzar, Grimm picked up one item of keen interest—the King believed that he had abducted Marie of Courland; and the girl herself was supposed to be deranged. It needed only this, to give Luther Grimm full cognizance of Count Otto's cards and how they had been played.

The affair was finished. Evrecourt led the bankers away, blandly insisting that the furious Pfalzar meet his other guests.

The courier departed in the berlin at full gallop. Luther Grimm handed Marie into his waiting carriage, and they left the music and the gay lights behind.

"Well, it's done!" exclaimed Marie. "It seems like a dream—and it's all over. What do we do now?"

"Hold our tongues." Grimm gestured toward the embassy driver. He gave an address at some little distance from the Hôtel de Paris. Upon reaching it, he dismissed the carriage, and they walked on to the little hostelry.

MADAME RUFIN herself admitted them. Luther Grimm had ordered supper prepared, and the good widow herself brought it to Marie's room, with old Jacques assisting. She departed; Jacques, beaming with delight, served them.

Here, for the first time, Grimm could relax. Here he was in safety. Madame Rufin was discreet and close-mouthed, and she also served France. She informed him that two men were waiting in his room. These were the two agents put at his disposal, and Grimm nodded. He sent them word that they should await him, and the widow departed.

"Now for you, Marie," he exclaimed. "You're all through here. I advise you to leave instantly. The city will be searched for us within another hour; tomorrow will be too late. I can get a carriage, and you can get off with Jacques—"

"Are you leaving?" she put in.

"I have work to do."

"Then I remain too," she said, watching him with radiant eyes.

Grimm reflected, and nodded. "After all, that might be the safest plan. They won't be certain whether we've gone or are still here…. Hm! At least, they'll be looking for you as you are. Can you change back to your man's costume? … Then do so, by all means. Do it the first thing in the morning, before you show yourself anywhere. Don't leave this house. I'll be off early. I must be at Potsdam by nine, to see the King."

"And suppose he puts you in prison?"

Grimm's eyes glittered. "A dozen Fredericks couldn't do that—with Mortlake here, with Osbrock at hand! St. Denis is not yet paid for in full. Also, I must settle matters with the King, clap a stopper on the lies Osbrock has told, and arrange the business of France. I've worked until now for my own country. Now I must justify the trust M. de Vergennes has put in me, and win Evrecourt's game for him. We'll see what Frederick says in the morning. So, my dear Marie, a last glass of wine and I'll be off. Here's to luck and beauty!"

In his own room, Grimm spoke briefly with the two French agents awaiting him.

"Count von Osbrock has a residence here?"

"Two, monsieur. One in the city, one just outside."

"Employ more men if you need them. Before noon tomorrow, I must know whether he has with him a one-eyed man. This man is English. He may have a cut or scar on his face."

They departed; and Grimm, thoroughly wearied, turned in. Achievement, achievement! Even in his dreams, this thought pushed him on. Now he had only to finish his work, round it off….

It was sharp nine of the clock, that next morning, when Frederick and two orderlies arrived at the inn below his Potsdam castle and the building where the corps of Pomeranian cadets were housed.

The King left his orderlies at the inn. Afoot, he ascended the path leading beside its famous closed and shuttered windows. It was now many years since Frederick, walking along that same path, had chanced to look in upon a beauty at her toilet; but the force of that shock was still reflected in the shuttered windows, never since opened.

Lean and agile despite his age, he mounted rapidly to the buildings above. His hat was old, dirty and comfortable. His frayed blue uniform with red facings was spattered on the breast with snuff, and he was in a vile temper, having placed the Marquis d'Evrecourt under arrest early that morning.

THE KING briefly inspected the quarters of his cadets—boys of fifteen, destined for future greatness. The rooms were almost bare of furniture. The beds were wretched; the few tables and chairs were of unpainted pine. One of the unhappy tutors occupying this monument to parsimony mentioned to the King that a gentleman was waiting to see him, and indicated a man strolling in the gardens.

Frederick presently entered the gardens and approached the loitering man, obviously a notary, who limped slightly and had a stoop. The King halted, swore lustily, and switched his patched boots with his stick.

"Who the devil are you?" he demanded at the top of his voice. "What are you doing here?"

The notary turned to him with a grin.

"Oh, hello! I suppose you're the gardener, eh? You needn't shout. I'm not deaf, thank heaven! I was cured of my deafness last year. When the devil will that unfortunate King of yours arrive? I'm tired of waiting for him."

"Oh, you are, eh?" barked Frederick. "You speak German like a fool."

"And you speak it like a Frenchman. Thank God, I'm no German!" retorted the notary angrily in French.

"Oh! That's different," Frederick said in the same language. "Why do you expect to see the King?"

"So you're French too!" The notary beamed. "No German could speak our language with such purity. And to think I took you for one of these rascally Prussians!"

The sharp gray eyes of the King softened. Nothing so pleased him as to be thought more French than the French.

"Come, answer my questions!" he said sharply. "Why do you call the King unfortunate? That's no way to speak of a great man like him."

LUTHER GRIMM chuckled. The part of a notary was his best rôle; hence he had chosen it for this occasion. He did not fear recognition from the King, but he knew that Berlin was humming with spies this morning.

"Well, just between you and me, this Frederick is damned unlucky in his friends and servants. Things go on that he doesn't know about. Like those officers of his getting killed day before yesterday at Wittenberg. And why? All because they wanted to cut the throat of that fellow Grimm."

Frederick's bitter features became positively livid.

"Grimm? You damned scoundrel, what are you talking about? What's this about officers?" He was shouting again.

Grimm snarled at him angrily: "Keep your names to yourself, or I'll report you to the King when he comes! Hm! It's like that man Grimm said to me—your doddering old King is played for a fool by the very men he trusts .the most."

"Grimm? Doddering old—*arrgh!*" exploded Frederick. "Listen to me, fellow! You're uttering words that'll put you behind the bars unless you explain them quickly, d'you hear?"

Grimm rubbed his unshaven chin and grinned.

"Aye, that's what Grimm said. I'm not afraid of the King, or you either. He told me they'd try to shut my mouth. This fellow Osbrock would do it quick enough, just as he sent those officers to shut Grimm's mouth."

Frederick eyed him keenly.

"I don't know whether you're a fool or a madman," he said slowly, "but I mean to find out. Osbrock, eh? See here, my man, I know the King very well indeed. I can help you with him. Tell me about these officers and this man Grimm."

"Of course, of course!" And the notary nodded amiably. "Well, I was at the tavern myself and saw it all. A big swaggering Norman, the Chevalier something—"

"Eh? The Chevalier de Castine—the best drill-officer in the army!"

"Right; that's the name. Then there was a queer man with a face like a skull, and a handsome Hungarian, a baron—"

"The finest cavalry leader in Europe!" exclaimed Frederick.

"Yes; I remember now; Osbrock got leave for them. Name of the devil! You must be telling the truth!"

"Of course I am. Didn't I see this man Grimm kill them one after the other? He tried to get out of it, but they were there to kill him. They were paid for it; they said so. Well, he killed them instead! And later, I had a talk with him—"

Frederick broke in with an air of stupefaction:

"Wait! Do you mean to tell me that three of the best swordsmen in the army were killed by one man?"

"Good God, are you deaf?" shouted Grimm angrily. "Of course they were. And it's—here's a funny thing—he wanted to see the King, too, and this Osbrock wanted him killed first. Something about a woman; he was accused of having kidnaped her, when Osbrock was the one who had done it. I don't know the details. He said he was bringing the woman to Berlin as proof of his story. She was in a carriage outside—a lovely woman, with the eyes of an angel—"

"Angels! Angels be damned!" Frederick began to stride up and down, lightning aflame in his eyes. "What devil's work have I chanced on here, eh? Damned if I like any of it. Osbrock, eh? Grimm—that *verdammte* interfering spy!"

"SPY?" ECHOED the notary vacantly. "Perhaps, perhaps; he seemed to know what he was talking about. He said they'd tricked the poor King, and I was to tell him so if I saw him."

"Tricked him?" Frederick swung around. "Who did? What about?"

"That nobleman with the queer name—Osbrock, that's it. Trying to keep the King from going to war with Austria. And there was something about money, too; about that woman who's supposed to be insane but who is nothing of the sort—"

A groan of furious chagrin escaped the King.

"Oh, you blasted idiot! For five minutes of clear-brained information, I—why, I'd give you anything! And you're a dunce. You can't talk."

Grimm straightened up.

"Is that a promise, Your Majesty?" he said in his natural voice.

Startled, the King stared at him.

"What the devil do you mean?" Anger and astonishment conflicted in the keen gray eyes. "Then you know me?"

"Yes, sire. No other man can curse so fluently as Frederick the Great." And Grimm's eyes twinkled. "Keep your word. Promise me immunity, a free pardon for M. d'Evrecourt—and I'll give you all the clear-brained information you can digest."

"So you've tricked me, eh?"

"Your pardon; I ask your forgiveness, sire. It's the only thing I have to ask from you—that, and your word of honor."

For a little space Frederick stood quite motionless, hands clasped on his stick, lips compressed.

"Very well," he said suddenly, brusquely. "You have my promise. Who are you?"

Grimm threw back his shoulders, removed hat and wig and spectacles, and bowed profoundly. It was no moment to be slack in respect.

"Luther Grimm of Philadelphia, Your Majesty. I think we've met before."

Frederick's bony old hands tightened over the knob of his stick until the knuckles stood out white. His nostrils dilated.

"By God, I should have you hanged and quartered—and I may do so yet!" he said slowly. "Let's see you keep your side of the bargain. Talk!"

Grimm talked.

He sketched the course of events from his first meeting with Marie of Courland, to the happenings of the past evening. He told how he had forced Evrecourt to his will; and at this, Frederick broke silence for the first time, with a rasping snort.

"You were given such authority? Damme if I'd give any man such powers! Produce it. Let's see the authority."

"Your Majesty, I burned it when it had served its need."

"She was taking you away, leaving me to the poison—and Mortlake seized her! What a joke on her!"

"Hm! Perhaps Vergennes isn't such a fool after all. Well, go on. I had the French embassy searched this morning. You have this woman hidden, eh?"

"Certainly, sire. She's not safe from Osbrock or her sister. And you should not have blamed poor Evrecourt. If you could have heard him sigh when Pfalzar threatened him with your anger—"

A croaking laugh broke from the King.

"I've promised you immunity, but not the woman. So Osbrock lied about her, eh? Told me she had offered me half her inheritance if I'd secure her in the balance—and he meant to take that for himself, eh? Well, I can still find her."

"Another man in your place, sire," said Grimm, "might still find her and wring out of her the balance of her inheritance; but you won't."

"Eh? Why not?"

"Because you've been saved from being made the dupe of England, the dupe of Austria, and the dupe of rascals. Also, because Your Majesty is one of the few men who are really kings by nature; and a king does not make war on women."

Frederick rasped: "No better reason?"

"Yes, sire. The sentiment of your heart, which you conceal from all eyes."

"You're a fool, a cursed fool!" snapped the King. "Do you really expect me to believe all this farrago of nonsense you've told me?"

Grimm bowed.

"I expect Your Majesty to prove the truth of it from Osbrock himself."

"Hm! I've heard the confession of your chief assistant, you rascal—one of the best secret agents in the French service, who knows your very thoughts! He has confessed everything to me. It's enough to hang you a dozen times over. I suppose you dare to proclaim this man a liar, eh? What's his name—Mortlake?"

Grimm, who had made no mention of the Englishman, was astounded.

"Mortlake? Your Majesty mistakes. Ask your own courtiers, your Marshal Keith, anyone! Mortlake has been an English agent for years—a free lance as well, serving anyone who paid him—a man whose entire life is given to getting money. Why, it was this man who led those three officers to Wittenberg to kill me! Ask the English ambassador here in regard to Mortlake, if you like."

It was Frederick's turn to be astonished. This reply, more than anything else, opened his eyes to the truth of Grimm's story.

Without a word more, as though unable to trust his own voice, the King turned his back and stalked stiffly away. The strange interview was ended.

Luther Grimm regained his waiting horse and spurred for Berlin. For good or ill, his work was done; and he was still alive and free.

As he rode, he began to realize how luck had played into his hand, in this interview. His spirits rose; triumph flooded into his heart. All was accomplished now. Count Otto was blocked, defeated, ruined; France was saved; the King's eyes were opened to the truth…. There remained—Marie.

IT WAS close to noon, when he strode into the little hostelry. Madame Rutin met him with blank, wondering gaze. His two secret agents were there, awaiting him; but Marie, said the widow, had left an hour ago. Grimm stared.

"Left? For where?"

"She did not say, monsieur," rejoined Madame Rufin. "She packed hastily and departed, with her servant Jacques."

"But how, how? Departed? It's incredible!" Grimm exclaimed. "Was she dressed as a woman?"

"No, monsieur—as a man."

"Quick! Summon those two men—"

The two agents yielded no information. Osbrock's country

house, they said, was closed, although the Countess von Osbrock was thought to be there. Osbrock himself was at his house in the city, and Mortlake was with him.

In the midst of Grimm's dismayed questions, Madame Rufin dragged in a chambermaid, who stammered out what she knew. There had been a caller for madame. A man with a carriage, a German, a servant of some kind. And here was a crumpled paper that had been left on the floor of the girl's room. The chambermaid had found it.

Luther Grimm seized it and stared at it, dumfounded. It was addressed to Marie: *"Come quickly with the bearer. Bring everything. —Grimm."*

It was not his writing; but Marie did not know his writing.

CHAPTER XII

NOON, OF the same day.
Count Otto von Osbrock, garbed in the richest of cut velvet from Genoa, his lace alone worth a fortune, and mounted on a Hungarian charger for which the King had once offered him five thousand thalers, rode into the courtyard of a small but elegantly appointed country house just outside Berlin.

"Is Her Highness here?" he asked the groom who came to take his horse.

"She has been out most of the morning, my lord, and has just returned. She is leaving again in a few minutes."

"If anyone asks for me, send him in at once."

With a pat to his little yellow mustache, Count Otto entered the house. While this was his property, it was used chiefly by his wife, who here retained certain servants of her own.

He entered a grand salon, furnished in the French fashion, where Flora sat writing. She greeted him gayly, eagerly.

"All goes well, Otto?" she inquired. "I haven't seen you since yesterday—"

"All has gone very badly," he returned in his calm, simpering fashion. He took a vial of perfume from his pocket and sniffed it delicately. "I've been canvassing my friends this morning, my dear Flora. It seems that I have none."

Her eyes sharpened. "What do you mean? What's happened?"

"The worst," he replied calmly. "I've ordered a carriage to be here in an hour, with my best horses—that is to say, the fastest horses in Prussia."

"Otto! You can't mean—why, it's impossible!" A shrill note came into her voice. "Tell me what's happened!"

"Calm yourself, my dear; this is no moment for excitement or for fainting-spells," he said. "Our friend Grimm has played the devil. Mortlake, who should have stopped him, bungled the job. I've dismissed Mortlake, by the way, from my employ. Last night, at the house of the French ambassador, your charming sister took over her inheritance. More correctly, she took half of it in bills-of-exchange on Paris, which have gone to M. de Vergennes. The balance is to be sent her there, within the month."

"*Oh!*" A short, sharp cry broke from Flora. "But that's—why, Otto, that's splendid! For us, the situation's better than ever!"

Count Otto eyed her curiously.

"You have a singular optimism," he observed gently, but with a trace of irony. "The King was furious about your sister, but failed to find her. An hour ago I met him as he was returning from Potsdam. I spoke to him; he gave me just one look, and passed me by. Evidently the worst has happened. Word has come from Vienna that the Emperor has rejected the ultimatum and is moving more troops into Bavaria. Failure on all sides, you see? I expect to be arrested at any time, but I've arranged to receive warning. Hence, the horses and carriage."

Flora studied him for a moment, a fleck of excitement in her lovely eyes.

"So you canvassed all your friends—and found none," she said in a low voice. "Did you expect to find one here?"

"That's for you to say, my dear." And Count Otto smiled. "I've told you the worst; there's nothing for it but flight. You need not share my failure, my disgrace. You can—"

"Perhaps I can retrieve it," she said slowly, thoughtfully.

HE LIFTED his head a little and met her intent gaze. A touch of warmth, of real feeling, came into his face.

"My dear Flora, I've never sufficiently appreciated you," he said in a quiet voice. "Most women would abandon the sinking ship; instead, you offer help! And such help as yours may be invaluable. I offer you my compliments, and my devotion. As a wife, you are magnificent."

"Never mind compliments," she said, almost brusquely. "You've lost your bid at power. Well, suppose we go back to Osbrock together? At least, the Rhineland is open to you, and your ancestral estates. If your game is lost here—begin another. I offer you wealth, which means power. A hundred million francs. It's yours."

His pale eyes kindled as he watched her. He forgot his affectation.

"A hundred millions! Are you in earnest?" he ejaculated. "Why, with such a sum we could put half Europe under our feet! But where is it to come from?"

She smiled slightly. "I've been at work this morning. Marie is locked up in the secret room; she's in man's costume. Her servant is tied up in the stables."

COUNT OTTO stared at her for one long moment. Then he leaped to his feet, transfigured with new energy.

"Where did you find her? How?"

"By chance. I saw her servant in the street; it was old Jacques, whom I knew well. I followed him, found where she was lodged. The rest was easy. But now, Otto, listen to me!" Her eyes hard-

"Tell me where Mortlake is, or you'll
be hanged within two minutes."

ened suddenly; her face chilled. "I offer you all this on one
condition alone—that you do not interfere with my plans."

"With all my heart! Whom do they concern?"

"This man Luther Grimm." As she uttered the name, a flash
passed through her lovely features—a flash of emotion as vivid,
as ominous, as terrible, as lightning. "Remember, no interfer-
ence! You've lost your game. I intend to play mine in my own
way."

He nodded, then glanced around as a lackey knocked and
entered.

"Excellency, a man with one eye is here. He demands speech
with you."

"So? Mortlake again, eh? And now he demands, does he?
Very well. Show him in at once." As the lackey bowed and
departed, Count Otto whipped a brass pistolet from under his
coat. He laid it in his lap, as he sat. "Quick, Flora! Into the
alcove, behind the curtains."

The woman rose and went to a window-alcove. She parted
the curtains and vanished behind them. They had scarcely ceased
moving when Mortlake was ushered into the room.

He came forward a step, saw the pistol in Count Otto's lap, and with a slight smile, bowed. Across his forehead was the cicatrice of a fresh, unhealed wound.

"Excellency," he said, "you dismissed me, but you forgot to pay me."

"Did you come here to get your money?" Count Otto sneered.

"That is all; I have need of it."

Count Otto put his hand into his pocket, drew out a purse, and tossed it to Mortlake. The latter caught it nimbly.

"Thank you. If you had not paid me, I would have killed you. However, you're a man of your word; good! Therefore we may once more be working together."

"Optimism Seems in the air this morning," observed Count Otto dryly. "May I inquire why you think we may once more be associated?"

"I've heard stories about that woman, this morning—your sister-in-law."

"All Berlin has heard stories today about Marie of Courland. Well?"

"Since I'm no longer in your employ," said Mortlake in his phlegmatic way, "I intend to catch her for myself, retrieve my failure, and perhaps you'll find it worth your while to join me in obtaining the half of her fortune that remains."

Count Otto chuckled amusedly.

"Your ambition does you credit, Mortlake," he said affably. "Very well; if you can manage it, by all means do so! Yes, she should be worth a hundred millions; and this time her bare signature will turn over the money. After the proper pressure has been exerted on her, of course. And now, perhaps, I may be relieved of your presence?"

The Englishman bowed and strode out of the room. Count Otto, with another chuckle, sniffed at his little vial.

"A damned dangerous rascal!" he said, as Flora appeared from behind the curtains. "He little dreams Marie is safely stowed away—eh?"

Flora, holding the curtains aside, beckoned. "Here, come to the window! Is that your carriage? The one that just drove in?"

Count Otto joined her, and his voice took on sharp anxiety.

"Yes, yes! And there's a messenger coming. Flora, I fear the worst; if it's arrest, we've no time—"

"Fear nothing, Otto," said she composedly. "Frederick won't arrest you—not when you know so many secrets. He'll merely banish you."

Count Otto made no response. A fine perspiration stood out on his forehead.

TWO MINUTES later the messenger was brought in, and handed him a sealed note. Count Otto tore it open, read it, and gave the man a coin.

"Tell your master," he said, "that I thank him for his kindness."

The messenger bowed and departed. Flora darted at her husband.

'Well? Well? What is it?"

"As always, my dear, you're right." Count Otto smiled. "The King has just signed a decree, declaring war against Austria, and moving every army corps—"

"But you, Otto! Never mind that. You!"

"I?" Count Otto flicked his lace handkerchief lightly. "Oh, I'm relieved of all authority. My property here is confiscated. I have forty-eight hours in which to get out of Prussia, on pain of arrest."

Her face lit up. "No worse? Good! Then we leave here tonight, and take our hundred million francs with us!"

"And our friend Luther Grimm?"

"That's my affair, not yours." Her eyes flashed. "Remember our agreement! You do your share; I'll give the orders this time. And no questions."

Count Otto shrugged.

"Very well, my dear. That man is the cause of all our troubles. My one regret is that he refused to come to terms with me."

"I don't intend to stop short with regrets," said Flora. As her husband met those beautiful but implacable eyes, he shivered slightly. "Now, I'm off. I have an important errand. I'll be back in less than an hour, for luncheon. *Au revoir!*"

"But," he broke in, "about leaving—"

"We don't leave until evening," she said curtly, and swished away.

LUTHER GRIMM, haggard and anxious, was pacing his room in the little Hôtel de Paris, when Flora von Osbrock was announced.

Grimm had accomplished nothing in the way of tracing Marie. His two agents had learned nothing; they were now engaging a dozen more trusty men. He had applied to the police, and the town residence of Osbrock had just been searched, to no avail.

He had learned of Osbrock's disgrace; it did not interest him. Mortlake seemed to have vanished bodily. The city was buzzing with wild rumors of war against Austria. Then, when Grimm heard that Flora was awaiting him in the hotel salon, he knew instantly that his search was ended. The mere fact that she knew where to find him, was eloquent.

Grimm walked in on her and closed the door behind him. She regarded him amiably, and he braced himself against the worst. Her smiling greeting, her radiant affability, told him enough.

"My dear Monsieur Grimm, I don't think we need mince words," she said. And she sighed. "Poor Otto! I've never seen a man so totally disheartened—"

Grimm surveyed her with icy eyes. "Never mind all that, madame. Where's Marie?"

Her brows lifted. "Would you really like to know? I don't think the rôle of a man suits her very well."

This was enough to prove everything. With an effort, he kept himself in hand.

"You, then, are responsible for her disappearance?"

"Yes."

The Countess, with this one word, abandoned mockery. She leaned forward, and made an imploring gesture.

"Listen, please! Marie is unharmed. You've beaten us, monsieur; your victory is complete and crushing. You're a hard and bitter man. My husband is ruined, broken, desperate. It's no longer a question of fighting, but of asking terms, of seeking our safety—"

"You seek it in a strange way, then," snapped Grimm. "By carrying off your sister!"

"That was before I knew the worst, before I knew you'd beaten us," she said. Anxiety and despair struggled in her lovely features. "But now that it's done—don't you see? It's our one chance. And I'm here to plead with you, to bargain. Otto will turn over this man Mortlake to you; he'll do anything you ask. I'll release Marie—"

"There's only one thing I want out of you and your husband," Grimm cut in harshly. "That's the chance to meet him sword in hand, and avenge the murder of my friend St. Denis."

"Very well; you shall have the chance," she said promptly.

Grimm eyed her.

"I don't believe a word you say. I suppose you have Marie at your house outside town, eh?"

She uttered a little ringing laugh. "Do you think I'd be so crude, when the police could trace me, when you could follow me, when the King himself has been trying to find her? Why, that would be the first place anyone would seek her."

"Wait." Grimm strode to the door. At his call, one of his two agents appeared. "Get word to the police instantly. Take what men you have, join the police, and search Osbrock's country place outside town."

The agent disappeared. Grimm swung back and eyed the Countess anew.

"We'll soon see."

"You can't find her when she's not there," Flora said composedly.

"Well, what do you want from me? Money?"

"No. Come out there this evening at seven—by that time you'll be satisfied that she's beyond your reach. We're leaving soon after; we must get out of Prussia at once. Otto has dismissed that man Mortlake. He wants your friendship—"

Grimm laughed harshly. "I've told you what I want from him."

"Very well. But now, tonight, let us get off safely. Listen! Otto has documents of the greatest value to France—copies of Frederick's negotiations with England, letters, everything! He has others at Osbrock. He'll hand them over to you. I'll release Marie. If you insist that he fight you, he'll do that later. But what we want, what we must have now, is a chance to get across the frontier!"

Despite himself, Grimm was impressed by her emotion. Her whole plea was quite illogical—but then, she was a woman.

"Suppose you release Marie here and now," he snapped.

"No! I can't do that until dark. The friends who are detaining her would become involved. I've promised to assure their safety. Come! Is it yes or no?"

Luther Grimm swiftly balanced her words. A trick? Perhaps. Fighting to save her husband? Perhaps. As he looked at her, he saw tears suffusing her eyes; she was watching him anxiously, desperately. Yes, the two of them were in panic, were ruined, were facing disaster. For Marie's sake, then—

"Done. I'll be there at seven," said Grimm. "But I'll not be alone, mind!"

"No matter. Otto fears you above everyone else. Let us get away from here, and you can have anything you ask."

With the simple words, she departed, leaving Luther Grimm almost convinced that he had chosen wisely.

THE COUNTESS drove home to her villa. There she gave swift orders. Not ten minutes later, Grimm's agent and a dozen police arrived with a warrant to search the premises. They searched, found nothing and no one to answer their search, and departed.

Count Otto and his wife stood at a window, watching the police ride off.

"Apparently you wish to keep me in the dark, my dear," said Osbrock mildly. She turned with a triumphant smile.

"Not now, Otto. Marie is in the secret chamber, off my room. That servant of hers is safely drugged and gone; he'll wake up tomorrow ten miles away. And at seven tonight you'll receive this man Grimm and talk terms with him."

"Eh?" Count Otto blinked. "I will?"

"Precisely. At that moment your carriage, with the fastest horses in Prussia, will be waiting behind the stables, at the back of the grounds by the little rear gate. At seven-thirty we'll be on our way—with Marie. True, Grimm will bring other men with him, but they'll be waiting in the courtyard. We'll slip out the back way to the stables and the carriage. Are you satisfied?"

Count Otto reflected. "No; but I foresee that this evening I shall be fully satisfied."

"Right!" A flash lit her radiant eyes. "I'll have Tokay wine for our guest when he comes. And I advise you not to drink from the bottle with the imperial seal. The rest, I leave to your imagination."

Count Otto looked at her for a moment; then his brows lifted.

"Oh!" he said thoughtfully.

THE DAY was overcast, with rain in the air; darkness came early.

The few of his possessions which Count Otto had been able

to pack, were bundled off in a carriage. As yet, the police had not arrived to confiscate everything here. His own carriage, with the best horses, were waiting behind the wall back of the stables, where the shrubbery concealed a little gate, seldom used and almost unknown to exist.

A few moments before seven Count Otto was sitting in the salon writing a letter, when his wife entered hurriedly.

"Quick, Otto—he's here!" she exclaimed. "Men with him, probably police. You receive him, bring him in. I'm going to the stables to make sure about the carriage and get Marie placed. My two men should be there, but we can take nothing for granted. Remember—be humble and agree to everything, promise everything! The wine's the thing."

"And no imperial Tokay for me," said Count Otto, with a smile.

Flora hurried through the house, and out into the night air by the rear. She crossed the gardens. A small stable building loomed dark and deserted, and she skirted this. Behind, the dark shrubbery loomed, and the gate. Through it she passed, to where the harnessed carriage stood waiting, a lantern lit but partially covered.

Two men were there, holding the spirited horses. Her own men, Russians, servants who had been with her for years, men whom she could trust implicitly.

"All's ready?" she breathed, low-voiced.

"All, highness."

"Good. You're leaving at once, with me. Count Otto is not coming. Go to the house, to my boudoir, and move aside the picture of my father. A keyhole is behind it; here's the key." She thrust it at them. Her voice was little more than a whisper, but instinct with energy. "My sister is there in the clothes of a man—you brought her this morning. In the secret chamber; you know the place. Bring her here. If she cries out, if she makes any resistance, silence her at all costs."

"Very well, highness. But we must tie these horses—"

"Give me the reins. I'll hold them," she exclaimed impatiently. "Hurry! Say nothing to Count Otto or anyone else. Return swiftly with her—we leave instantly!"

The two men slipped away.

Countess Flora, at the horses' heads, held them, patted them, spoke soothingly. The lantern was on the ground close by. The shawl fell away from her pale gold hair; her face stood out in the dim light of the lantern like some old cameo, her features distinct, beautiful, perfect.

There was a stir in the shrubbery, and with a startled question, the Countess turned. A man appeared, three others behind him; as she fled toward the gate, two figures were beside her in a flash. One low cry escaped her lips, unheard.

Meantime, in the courtyard of the villa, a score of horsemen halted and dismounted. Some were police, others were Grimm's men.

Two lackeys, with ready torches aflare, opened the doors. Count Otto appeared there in the ruddy flickering light, and bowed as Grimm came up the steps. Grimm turned and flung an order at the men below.

"Guard the gates; let no one leave. If I call, be ready to enter." He turned and looked at Count Otto. "Good evening to you. I've come as arranged."

"Enter, and welcome," said Count Otto affably. "Madame is dressing, I believe; but our discussion may proceed without her."

He led Grimm into the big salon, now in a soft glow of light from candles set in massive silver sconces. Ignoring the invitation to be seated, Grimm stood glancing about, alert and suspicious. His gaze came to rest on Count Otto, who met that intent look and gestured helplessly.

"Monsieur, what's past is past," he said gently.

"But must be paid for," was Grimm's harsh comment.

Count Otto bowed.

"I'm in no position to deny, apologize, or refuse. I'm like a swordsman who has been disarmed and is at the mercy of his opponent, monsieur."

"Not yet, but I trust soon," said Grimm implacably.

HE PAUSED, as the doors were thrown open. A lackey entered, bearing a silver tray which he deposited on the table. The tray bore curious and delicate goblets of Venetian glass, and two dusty bottles. When the lackey was gone and the doors were closed again, Count Otto broke silence.

"Monsieur, I stand ready to make you every amend in my power for what is past. I have an entire *dossier* of diplomatic documents ready to turn over. The man Mortlake is in security, and I can place him in your hands—"

"Devil take him and your documents," broke in Luther Grimm. "I want Marie of Courland, alive and unhurt; and I want you to answer to me for the murder of St. Denis."

"Agreed. Wherever and whenever you like. We may arrange the time and place this evening. It must be beyond the Prussian frontier, however. If by some accident I were hurt and detained on Prussian soil, I'd be imprisoned."

Grimm nodded. This was fair enough. "You'll not be hurt. You'll be killed," he said curtly.

"Ah! In that, we differ." Count Otto looked at him with a smile, and moved to the table. He touched one of the bottles reverently. "Tokay from the imperial cellars! A toast together. By the way, my wife has sent for Marie; she'll be here very shortly."

AS HE poured wine into the goblets, he paused midway, to bend an earnest look on Luther Grimm.

"I don't pretend, monsieur, that we go out of this room friends. No, I'll not play the hypocrite. I've had my day. I've played for high stakes, and lost. And yet you, who have won, can afford to be generous. I appealed to you once before—"

"And you murdered my friend," said Grimm uncompromisingly. He watched Count Otto pour into one glass from a plain bottle. The other bottle had a leaden seal dangling from a ribbon. "Not to mention what happened in the Wittenberg tavern."

"You have no reason to complain about that." And Count Otto laughed a little. "However, I lost; I'm ready to grant whatever satisfaction you seek. We can discuss the matter like gentlemen."

Negligently, he extended the glass which he had filled from the imperial bottle. Grimm shook his head.

"Thanks, no. Pour me another, from the same bottle you're sampling. It might be safer."

Count Otto's brows lifted.

"Oh, I see! Upon my word, you suspect me, eh? Very well."

He put aside the two goblets, and poured two others from the plain bottle. One of these he lifted to his lips and emptied, then refilled the glass. Grimm accepted the other.

COUNT OTTO took up his glass again, and sniffed it. His smoothly powdered features betrayed not the least indication of dismay or confusion. After all, this was his wife's game. If the American had been too sharp to chance poisoned wine, let her get out of it as best she could.

"It's obvious that I could scarcely poison you without sharing your fate," he observed dryly. "To the future—to our mutual satisfaction!"

Grimm touched glasses, and sipped the Tokay, which was admirable.

"I'll ride to the frontier with you," said Grimm. "Once across, we can pause and settle matters. I intend to kill you as you killed St. Denis—but without a trick."

Count Otto shrugged, and emptied his glass again.

"The opportunity shall be yours," he said amiably. "It will be a pleasure to kill you, in some ways; and yet I shall regret doing it. I still think that if we were to work together—well, we shall see. May I refill your glass?"

*Figures appeared, leaping forward; they were all
around him of a sudden. Grimm's rapier drove
at one man desperately, and ran him through.*

Grimm, who had scarcely tasted the wine, shook his head,
then drank the rest of the contents of his glass.

"I came here for action, not wine. Where is the Countess?"

"Slow, like all women, at dressing. Marie should arrive at any
moment. Flora has not harmed her in the least—"

"If there's been any attempt to force a signature out of her,"
Grimm said coldly, "neither one of you will leave this place as
you expect."

Count Otto shook his head. "No. I think Flora had such an
idea at first, but she abandoned it. If—"

He turned sharply. The doors were flung open, and a man
appeared. He was one of the two Russians who served the
Countess. He looked agitated, and held a paper in his hand.

"Pardon, your highness," he said to Count Otto. "May I have
a word with you?"

"You may not," lashed out Grimm's voice. "If you've anything to say, say it in front of me."

Count Otto made a gesture of assent. The man came forward, stammering.

"Highness, the carriage! It is gone. Madame sent us for—for the young lady. We came back with her—the carriage was gone. We found this by the lantern." And he extended the paper to Count Otto, who snatched at it.

"What's all this?" demanded Luther Grimm with quick suspicion. "What carriage?"

"My carriage; it was to take us away." Count Otto passed one hand across his forehead. "Upon my word—here, read this, Grimm! That man says he has made off with her, with Marie! I don't understand it—"

Grimm seized the paper from his hand. The words written there were venomous:

> *Thanks for the carriage, Count Otto, and the horses, and the young lady. If you wish to take me back as an associate, and to discuss that hundred million francs, I'll be at the Inn of the Last Virgin. So will your sister-in-law.*
>
> *Mortlake.*

An inarticulate cry broke from Grimm, dimly comprehending what it meant.

A groan silenced him, brought him around. To his amazement, Count Otto had risen and was standing with an expression of wild horror frozen in his eyes.

"Tricked me—she tricked me!" His voice was choked, agonized, hoarse. "I see it now—the she-devil has tricked me! She said one bottle was poisoned; she lied, she lied! They were both poisoned—both of them. She meant it for me—"

With another groan, Count Otto fell back into his chair, and death stood in his graying face.

CHAPTER XIII

L UTHER GRIMM wakened with a rush from that
one frightful instant of realization and horror. He leaped
to the nearest window, smashed it out, and his voice lifted.

"In here—help! Search the gardens. Bring in everyone you
find. Arrest every person here—"

Then, desperately conscious of the glassful of Tokay he had
swallowed, he was retching frantically, forcing himself to get
that poison out of his stomach before it went into his system.
Luckily, it was only a moment or two since he had drunk the
wine. Count Otto had been far ahead of him there, and had
also taken double the quantity.

Voices, booted feet, stormed through the house. Men scattered about the gardens; lanterns and torches flared, excited
cries rose from everywhere. Grimm was conscious that one of
his own men had appeared and was assisting him. Then he felt
pain taking hold of him in short sharp spasms.

His mind remained clear enough. So Mortlake had somehow
taken Marie and fled for it—fled to the Inn of the Last Virgin!
A sharp game of his own, that!

COUNT OTTO sat with his head sunken, his eyes closed.
Spasmodic tremors passed through his body from moment to
moment. Luther Grimm got on his feet and began to walk up
and down rapidly, his agent assisting him. He was fighting off
the pain. Thank heaven he had delayed drinking that wine!

Count Otto lifted his head slightly. His eyes opened and
fastened on the American; a hopeless and terrible agony was
in their depths. He tried to say something, and could not.
Grimm halted and eyed him coldly.

"So you tried to poison me, eh? And fell into your own trap.
Well, I hope you enjoy it! Think of St. Denis as you die."

Two of the police, at last comprehending the situation, had

taken charge and were bringing order out of chaos. Now came a burst of voices, a rush of footsteps, and into the big room shoved a clump of figures. A harsh German voice cried out excitedly:

"Excellency! We found this fellow by the stables, with his hands bound—"

Grimm stared incredulously at the cloaked figure they pushed forward. His heart leaped. A cry broke from him.

"Marie! You here!"

He flung himself at her, seized her hands, peered into her face. Yes, it was Marie in her man's attire, brows and hair blackened, a hat pulled over her head; she clung to him, uttering half-hysterical words, in fright, bewilderment and joy. Grimm caught and held her close.

"It's all right, my dear, all right! But where's Mortlake? How did you—"

She drew back, startled. "Mortlake? I haven't seen him." Her eyes fell on the group of servants being gathered in one corner. "There—those two men! They came and brought me out of the house. They said I was going away with my sister. But she was gone. There was no carriage waiting. Nothing but a sheet of paper on the ground—"

The two Russians were sharply, swiftly questioned. They blankly admitted everything, yet were obviously lost in astonishment. The Countess had been holding the horses when they left. When they returned with Marie, she was gone, the horses were gone, the carriage was gone—only the lantern and that letter which one of them had brought in to the Count.

A sudden silence fell. Grimm's blood chilled. Upon the room lifted a laugh, so horrible and croaking that it seemed like laughter out of hell.

Count Otto had come to his feet. He stood swaying, clutching at the air, his face contorted in that ghastly burst of mirth. Words came from him, on the wings of death.

"So that's it—ho-ho! She was taking you away, leaving me

to the poison—and Mortlake seized her—ho-ho-ho!" The spasm of eerie laughter shook him anew. "What a joke on her! Mortlake took her for you—didn't know you were dressed as a man—"

He coughed suddenly, lost balance, and collapsed. His out-flung fingers clawed at the carpet, once, twice; then they relaxed and were motionless.

The chill of horror that seized on Grimm was loosened by comprehension. Those words explained everything. He led Marie to a seat across the room, away from the dead man, away from the police and the crowding domestics. She shivered and clutched his arm.

"What does it all mean? I thought you had sent for me. Instead, it was she—my sister—ugh! I dared not eat anything. I knew she'd drug me, as she did once before. I've been here all day—"

"Here in this house?" Grimm exclaimed. "Impossible! The police were here, searching it."

"There's a secret chamber. But where is she? What did he mean?"

Luther Grimm explained in brief words, himself gaining fuller understanding as he spoke with her.

"But Jacques!" she exclaimed suddenly. "He was with me. What did she do with him? Find out, quickly! They took him away—"

Grimm interrogated the two Russian servants of Flora. They talked readily enough. The old servitor had been drugged and taken out into the country. They pointed out the groom who had done it, and presently that man was riding off between two of Grimm's agents.

In another ten minutes Luther Grimm, with the last of his slight pain gone and few ill effects left, was being driven into the city, with Marie beside him. He was silent as he drove. Where to, Luther Grimm? The question reëchoed in his brain. It recurred on the ride back, at the hotel, through the eager greetings of Madame Rufin, in Marie's room as the good widow served some supper for them.

Where to, Luther Grimm? He asked himself the question anew.

Marie met his gaze and smiled whimsically, tenderly.

"Where to now, Luther Grimm?"

He started. Strange that she should thus repeat his own mental query!

"Where to? That's it," he said. "First, the Inn of the Last Virgin, to even the score with this scoundrel Mortlake. After that—well, I don't know. I've finished my work for France; now America calls me. We've a hard fight there yet."

"But first, Paris," she said. "Why not together?"

Why not, indeed? His dark blue eyes kindled as they rested on her. She met the look, and her soft color mounted.

"Why not America?" he said, and his whimsical smile leaped out at her. "Paris first, then. But I've work to do on the way!" His jaw set hard and stubborn for a minute. "And it's no work for a woman," he added.

"Fair enough. Take a comrade, then; you may have use for one. And I'll keep this man's costume for a bit."

Grimm gave her a quick, sharp look.

"Done with you," he said. "We'll get away from here by to-morrow noon. Agreed?"

"Agreed. But,"—and her face became anxious—"how about my sister? I don't pretend to love her; but when I think of her in the hands of Mortlake—"

Grimm laughed harshly. "No, think, rather, of Mortlake in her hands! Never fear. By this time he's discovered his mistake. And remember, they'll think Count Otto dead, and me with him! They'll not be sure. They'll wait at the Last Virgin for word—and they'll get it. Good night to you!"

And rising, he was gone quickly to his own room.

EARLY IN the morning, Grimm found that old Jacques had returned safely. He sent a note to the French ambassador, with certain requests. As the morning wore on, he had finished his preparations, had made what purchases he needed, and was scribbling a report to Dr. Franklin, to go by courier, when a lackey brought him a laconic note:

"Come quickly.—Evrecourt."

Grimm obeyed the summons instantly.

Upon reaching the embassy, he was taken at once to the study of the marquis. Evrecourt greeted him warmly, but with an oddly embarrassed hesitation.

"Well?" said Grimm cheerfully. "What makes you look so uneasy? Haven't you patched things up with the King?"

"Oh, that! Yes, yes. In fact I've just come from the palace." The ambassador regarded him with a wary eye, askance. "Here are the passports for Mademoiselle Marie and her servant. The carriage is ready, as you requested; you must have seen it as you entered. *Mon Dieu!* What a morning—what a rush and a scramble! The Austrian ambassador has been dismissed. Frederick is moving all troops instantly. He himself is leaving or has already gone, to take command of the army."

GRIMM GLANCED at the documents. "I don't see a passport here for me."

"No. Devil take it, Grimm, you must be patient about this! The King was in one of his furious, insane rages. He had just written an order for your arrest. By this time the police are probably seeking you—"

Grimm stared. "What? My arrest? Why, it's impossible! He himself promised me immunity!"

"I know. He spoke of his promise; he says he'll keep it later, but for the present you're too dangerous to be left at large. He merely wants to have you available. Now, for the love of heaven accept the matter gracefully!" pleaded Evrecourt in haste, seeing the look on Grimm's face. "He means you no harm; I believe he wants to offer you some employment. Things are ticklish for all of us. With war declared, every frontier post will be closed. You can't possibly hope to leave Berlin, and the King—"

"Bedamned to him!" Grimm exploded hotly. "I should have remembered the ingratitude of princes! A promise is nothing to him, as against policy. Can't leave, eh? By heaven, I'll leave in spite of a dozen kings! Get one of your lackeys here—on the jump!"

The nervous ambassador obeyed.

Five minutes later, Luther Grimm was attiring himself in the livery of the astonished lackey. He clapped the curled wig on his head, crammed the tricorne hat over it, and snapped a curt demand.

"Have that carriage brought around, instantly! Take my letter for Franklin and send it by your next courier. Money? Thanks, I've plenty. This disguise will get me out of Berlin. I still have my old passport in the name of Jan Stern; it'll take me across the frontier."

"But, my dear fellow, I tell you—"

"Tell me nothing. Get that carriage around!"

In a gale of fury, Grimm left the embassy on the box of the carriage, and drove around to the Hôtel de Paris. As he drew rein, Jacques appeared. He came quickly to Grimm's call, with dismay in his wrinkled features.

"Monsieur! The police are inside! They're asking for you—"

"Never mind. Get your mistress here, quickly. We're off."

They were off, indeed—the luggage loaded in, Marie and her servant inside the carriage, Grimm driving, while two agents of police looked placidly on. The livery of the French ambassador was well known.

Grimm applied the whip, and the horses leaped away. On through the city streets, now all in tumult with tokens of war— couriers and aides at the gallop, troops on the move, artillery rumbling and clanking along. On to the city gates,—but here Grimm's heart sank.

He came upon a traffic blockade. Squads of grenadiers were

drawn up, officers were checking all who came or went. Somehow Grimm got his carriage through the press to the gates, only to find two soldiers coming to the heads of the horses, and an officer barking at him.

"Unload yourselves and go back! All horses are commandeered for army use."

"At your peril!" stormed Grimm furiously. "This is the carriage of the French ambassador. These are his horses!"

"Take that up with the lord marshal," the officer broke in arrogantly.

Grimm came to his feet. His whip lashed down, and again. With a yell and an oath the officer fell back. The horses jumped in frantic pain, the soldiers scattered. Down came the whip again. The carriage lurched forward; with the horses in a wild gallop, the gates were passed.

Shouts and tumult arose. A sudden crash of muskets rang out. Another volley, and balls were whistling around. Luther Grimm swayed uncertainly, regained balance, and clung to the reins. His hat flew off. His wig fell away and was gone on the rush of air. He sank back on his seat, with blood running down his head from a bullet-furrow.

But the carriage went on in mad career, outrunning any possible pursuit.

CHAPTER XIV

ONCE AGAIN the notary Jan Stern, stooped and black-clad, spectacles on his nose, traveled the highways unregarded and alone. He passed the Prussian frontier in a crowded diligence, and if there were a bandaged head under his wig, it only served the better to disguise Luther Grimm of Philadelphia.

Marie of Courland had parted from him, had struck on ahead of him with important work to do. Having her own passport from the hand of Frederick, she was in no peril.

INTO COBLENZ came the notary, still traveling by diligence. He had far outrun any news of Count Otto's death, and Osbrock's police were undoubtedly still searching for Luther Grimm, so he took no chances whatever.

He put up at the Fürstenhof once more, and found a note awaiting him from Marie:

> *I've seen Hoffman. All arranged. Cavaignac and the other men you want are with me. Will await you at Alken.*

A long night's sleep, and Luther Grimm took the public diligence once more for Alken and Osbrock.

Of an evening, in time for early dinner, he alighted with the other passengers at the post tavern in Alken, the place where he had fought his way to freedom.

As he stood looking around, memories flooding back on him, he saw old Jacques approaching with a smile.

"Monsieur! I've been watching each arrival. Give me your bundle. We have rooms here. You're not far behind us."

Grimm followed him, to the presence of Marie; and the warmth of her greeting lifted Grimm to swift happiness. In joyous energy, he flung aside his disguise.

Ahead, only a few miles distant, lay the Inn of the Last Virgin.

"I see you're all right again—your head has barely a scar." Smiling as she regarded him, Marie poured wine. "We have had no trouble. Hoffman was splendid, and provided the men without question. They're here now. Shall I send for them?"

"If you will."

She dispatched Jacques; in a few moments six men came into the room.

Grimm knew Cavaignac, a bluff and hearty man, one of the best agents in the French employ. The other five were Cavaignac's men; all knew of Luther Grimm, eyed him curiously, greeted him with delighted respect.

"We should send to the Last Virgin," said Grimm. "We must learn how things are going there."

Marie laughed a little. "I sent Cavaignac there last night. He just returned an hour ago. My sister has one of the best rooms at the inn; she's not stopping at the castle. Mortlake discovered his mistake, evidently."

"And Mortlake?" Grimm asked of Cavaignac. "The one-eyed man is there?"

"Yes, monsieur. Also two grooms, one hostler, eight horses in stalls. Three serving-women and a cook. The big man who runs the place, Master Rudolph, and his wife. Also, four soldiers from the castle, who live in the stables or the caverns behind the stables."

"A good report. Did they know you for a Frenchman?"

"Not at all, monsieur. I am a Silesian horse-dealer." And Cavaignac grinned. "The lady and the one-eyed man reached there two days ago. She has been ill; she had some sort of fit or fainting-spell."

Grimm flung Marie a glance, remembering that scene in the Dortstadt tavern.

"You saw this man Mortlake?"

"Certainly, monsieur. His orders are obeyed there."

Grimm looked at Marie, frowningly.

"They've some game afoot—you'll see! That devil Mortlake doesn't bide quiet for nothing. They're waiting to hear whether Count Otto's dead or not, whether it's known she poisoned him."

"One thing more, monsieur," Cavaignac said. "On top of the inn is a cresset, a huge iron basket filled with combustibles. Once alight, it can be seen from the castle, smoke by day, fire by night. A signal."

Grimm nodded. "That cresset must not be lighted. By heaven, I'll give 'em a different sort of signal before I'm through! You have horses?"

"Everything."

"Sword and a brace of pistols for me, and a horse. Be ready in fifteen minutes. I'll give you orders on the way."

Cavaignac saluted and led out his men. Marie turned quickly to Grimm.

"You're not going there now, tonight?"

"We'll be off before dark." Grimm's harsh features were alight. "I can't sleep with that work so close and still undone."

"Then I'll go with you."

"You'll not," he said, and met her gaze. "Jacques will drive you over later. Follow in an hour, and I'll be through by then. No argument."

She attempted none. Those eyes were chill. Grimm's thoughts were reflected in his face—thoughts of St. Denis nabbed there, of the French groom who had been hanged, of this evil nest he had sworn to root out. And Mortlake waiting there.

"And Flora?" said Marie, after a little. "Remember, she's still my sister."

"I don't fight women." Grimm's laugh was curt and mirthless.

The meal came to an end. In the courtyard, the horses were ready, the men waiting. Grimm turned to Marie.

"Luck go with you!" she said simply. "We'll follow in an hour."

He looked into her eyes. Suddenly a quick, gay laugh came to his lips; he caught her to him, and swiftly kissed her.

"Good-by, my dear! Follow me in an hour—not before."

He was gone; and with him rode the memory of his kiss returned....

Darkness was falling as they clattered out of Alken, Cavaignac beside Luther Grimm, the five men following. Grimm had sword at his hip, pistols at his saddle.

"Orders?" he replied to Cavaignac's question. "Tell off two of your men to collect the women at the inn and hold them under guard; two more to take care of the grooms and hostler. You and the fifth man, remain with me. We'll get there before midnight, if we ride fast."

*Mortlake, still
gripping his bloody
knife, dragged
himself forward inch
by inch, his dilated
eye unwaveringly on
the figure of Grimm.*

"What do you intend?"

"To pay a debt," said Luther Grimm.

H E   S T R U C K   into a reckless, relentless pace in the darkness. There was no moon, and starlight was not enough for these roads. Cavaignac protested, but Grimm rode even faster. Something tugged at him, pricked him into speed.

"A horse has gone down," lifted the voice of Cavaignac.

Grimm spurred the harder. One man had dropped behind. Another fell out, as they came to a crossroads and a dark object against the stars. It was the gibbet of Osbrock. Almost there now!

The castle loomed dark, the hamlet below was dark. Midnight was nearing. They came within sight of the Last Virgin, and an oath broke from Grimm. Lights there, torches glimmering from the courtyard. Lights at this hour? Why? He checked his mad course.

"Rein in, Cavaignac! Let me go in first. You follow. Use your steel if they resist—and let no one reach that cresset, mind!"

The courtyard widened before him. Cavaignac and the three remaining men fell back. Luther Grimm rode on, and sent his horse into the courtyard, then drew rein.

Before him in the ruddy glare of torches stood a carriage; two grooms were putting horses in harness. They stared at him, slack-jawed. From the inn came forth a burly figure—Master Rudolph.

"A guest? You're late on the road, highness," he exclaimed, coming up to Grimm. "Well, better late than never, as the saying goes—"

"True for you," said Grimm, and swung the heavy pistol he was holding by the barrel.

The blow was merciless. Master Rudolph groaned to the crushing weight of it, and collapsed in his tracks. Into the courtyard surged Cavaignac and his men; they dismounted, swords flashing. A yell broke from one of the grooms:

"The signal, Claus—quick, the signal!"

A figure was already flitting over the cobbles toward the stairs. Cavaignac met it with a sword-flash, and the hostler fell sprawling.

"Light it yourself! Look out for—"

The two grooms were leaping for the stairs. Grimm ran one of them down, caught up with him, and his sword brought the man down. The other, whipping out a knife, stabbed savagely, shouting the alarm until he died. From somewhere within rose shrieks and the voices of women.

"Two of you—in there!" snapped Cavaignac. "Silence those women. Lock 'em up. Next, captain?"

"Guard the stables. Take your pistols—look out for the men there!"

Grimm was already on the stairs. That carriage being harnessed showed how truly he had been guided to speed. Countess Flora, of course; she and Mortlake would be departing. As

Grimm came to the head of those outside stairs, he looked down to see the last two of his party come into the courtyard. He called:

"That big fellow there—tie him up, bind him fast! Then help Cavaignac."

He himself wanted no help. Here were the inn rooms before him—and yet, as he advanced, the corridor ahead showed empty. A half-open door showed a glimmer of candle-light. He went to it and kicked it wide. The room was empty. Woman's garb was scattered about—it was the room of the Countess.

Grimm caught up the candle and went from room to room. No other guests were here; no one was here.

PRESENTLY GRIMM descended the stairs into the courtyard. He glanced at the men last arrived. They stood over the bound and senseless Master Rudolph.

"Drag him over to the horse-trough and revive him," said Grimm.

Cavaignac approached; a brisk and efficient fellow, Cavaignac.

"The women accounted for and locked in," he reported briskly. "My three men are guarding the stables. No one else about the place. No sign of the four soldiers who were here yesterday. The two grooms are dead, the hostler dying."

"Did you find any entrance from the stables to underground chambers?"

"Yes; a big double door's there, closed and locked. My men are watching it."

GRIMM WALKED over to where Master Rudolph, still bound, was gasping and spluttering. The two men hauled him to his feet. He looked at Luther Grimm, looked again—and shrank back in terrified recognition.

"Where's the Englishman, Mortlake?"

"I—I don't know, highness—"

"Speak up, Master Rudolph," said Luther Grimm deliberately. "Count Otto is dead, poisoned by his wife, who's here with Mortlake. I owe you something, but I'll forgive you the debt for information. Tell me where Mortlake is, or you'll be hanged within two minutes."

Master Rudolph gaped.

"Dead—poisoned? *Herr Gott!* You say the Countess did it?"

"She did," said Grimm with chill precision.

"They—in the caverns, highness. They went in together. They were about to leave here—"

"The caverns? What did they go in there for?"

"Money. The Englishman had an order from Count Otto to take charge of the money that's kept inside there. The Countess had witnessed it—*Gott!* You say she poisoned him? That woman—"

"Gag this man. Leave him bound," ordered Grimm.

And he watched it done. Money, eh? It all was clear in a flash. Treasure was kept there under the hillside. Greed was the driving urge of Mortlake. He and the Countess Flora, a forged order for that money—taking to flight? Fleeing outside Germany entirely, to separate!

"Come to the stables," ordered Grimm, and led the way, sword in hand. Cavaignac and the other two followed. Three men waited there.

One of the ruddy torches was brought. They were standing in the stables now; at the back of them, the smoky light showed the outlines of a huge double door, heavily bound with iron. Grimm's brain flashed back to all the rumors and Wild tales he had heard about the Osbrock caverns at the back of this inn. But why were these doors closed? And they were fastened on this side.

"Odd," said Grimm, frowning. "They are getting out treasure of some kind. Then why close these doors?"

"There might be another entrance—"

"Right, right!" Grimm's face cleared. "Go ahead. Open up

these doors; sweep this place clean. Take your pistols and four men—leave one here with me."

Cavaignac led his men at the doors. A bolt shot back, and they slowly swung open on creaking hinges. A stable lantern was lighted from the torch. Cavaignac took the lantern and the torch was thrust into a sconce and left there to furnish light for Grimm.

Cavaignac and his men started into a wide passage which pierced into the very heart of the hillside. To right and left were doors in the stone walls. All of these stood half ajar. Grimm, gazing after the party, saw Cavaignac halt and hold up his lantern.

The way was blocked by two doors—one to the right, one to the left. After a momentary hesitation, Cavaignac chose that to the left. It swung open. His light flickered on past it and was lost to sight. The echoing footsteps died away; the passage was in blackness.

"Keep watch," said Grimm to the one man left with him. "If the people we want are in there, they may break cover from some other entrance."

"Look!" exclaimed the man. "That fellow we bound—"

From where they stood, they had a clear view of a portion of the courtyard. Master Rudolph was flinging himself to right and left, frantically striving for freedom. Inarticulate noises came from his gagged jaws. Grimm, who had seen those ropes well tied, laughed shortly.

"He's safe enough. Go get the torch. We'd better look through the stables for other openings into the caverns."

The man went to get the torch from its holder, ten feet away.

IN THE stalls, the horses were stirring uneasily, snorting, plunging. Grimm, his eyes straining at the obscurity, Was conscious of queer faint sounds. He took alarm, and swung around.

"Quick with that torch—"

His voice failed. The man was reaching for the torch, reaching up toward it, but his extended hand was merely clawing, tearing at the stable wall in desperate agony. No sound whatever came from him. Clear in the torchlight, something stood out of his back. It was the haft of a long knife, a knife that transfixed him, pinning him to the wooden partition. Suddenly his arm fell.

"All right," sounded a voice. "Take him!"

Figures appeared, leaping forward in the ruddy light. A shout broke from Grimm; useless! They were all around him of a sudden. One man darted in, and Grimm's rapier drove at him desperately and ran him through.

A choking cry escaped Luther Grimm. Something clutched at him and bore him backward, something else. He struck out vainly. These men had long pikes, eight-foot pikes; two of them held him pinned against the stable wall, the sharp prongs nipping him, the men far beyond his reach. The third pike slashed in, struck his sword, knocked it from his hand as he was held helpless, his coat torn off.

Then Mortlake appeared, laughing.

CHAPTER XV

LUTHER GRIMM stood firmly held, unable to move lest the pike-points rip into him; the ghastly consciousness of his frightful position was stupefying.

Mortlake moved forward, reached up past the dead man hanging on the knife, and took the torch from its socket. That knife, as Grimm now realized, must have been hurled with terrific force. Carrying the torch, Mortlake approached Grimm and held up the light, his one eye ablaze with triumph.

"Get a fresh torch, one of you," he ordered, and his voice was very calm. "This will be burned out soon."

Except in his flaming eye, he displayed no emotion, ho exultation. He met the furious panting gaze of Luther Grimm with unmoved features. The third of his men dropped his pike and went running for another torch. These three, and the one whom Grimm had struck down, were soldiers from Osbrock's castle—the same four Cavaignac had seen here the preceding day.

Nothing moved here; yet in the silence Grimm heard a rustle and a quick, light step. The one eye of Mortlake shifted, followed some object across the courtyard—Grimm, unable to see, knew that this must be the Countess Flora. Then Mortlake looked at him again and spoke.

"You were looking for me, eh? Well, you've found me—and I've found you. Steady with those two pikes!"

Grimm said nothing. The steel points were into him, pricking him with firm pressure; any movement, and they would thrust through him. He remembered the stamping restless horses. Mortlake and his men had emerged from the caverns by another entrance into the stables; it was very simple.

Now the man sent for a fresh torch came running back with it. Mortlake lit it from the first, which he then thrust back into its wall socket. Holding up the fresh light, he motioned to the man.

"While they hold him here, get rope. Tie his hands up to those harness hooks, and stretch them well out."

Turning, Mortlake held up his torch and moved rapidly into the wide opening of the passage. The gaze of Grimm followed him, as he went straight back to where those two doors blocked the passage. He closed the left-hand door, that through which Cavaignac and his men had gone, slid a massive bar across it, and returned.

Meantime, with a length of rope, the third man bound Grimm's left arm to one of the huge hooks along the partition, then his right arm. Grimm said nothing, attempted no resistance. Mortlake nodded as the two pikes were lowered.

"Lay aside the pikes," he said. "All's safe now. The others are caught inside there and we needn't worry about them."

Spots of blood came out on Grimm's shirt, but he was conscious of no pain.

Mortlake moved to the figure of the man hanging on the wall, took hold of the knife, and wrenched it free. The body slumped down. Mortlake wiped the knife, and put it out of sight. Then he came back to Grimm.

"To think of you being here—why, you must be the devil himself!" he exclaimed slowly, with a certain mild astonishment. He turned to the three men. "Where is the Countess? Where did she—"

They looked around. One of them uttered a sharp word. Another pointed. There was a stir in the courtyard; the carriage began to move. A whip lashed at the horses and they plunged forward. The carriage lurched and rattled out of the courtyard.

A LOW laugh came from Mortlake. "So she's gone, eh?" His calm seemed inflexible. "Well, so much the better. You men, wait here until I come back. Watch this man sharply; if he tries to talk, kill him. Remember that, Grimm! If you want to die, talk to these men, bribe them, use your tongue. You men, kill him at the first word!"

He swung around and started back into the passage. Grimm watched him go.

Obviously, Cavaignac and his men were securely captured. They had come back to the the closed left-hand door and were attacking it. Faint sounds were heard, echoes of a futile assault, the muffled reports of pistols. Mortlake, his torch up, examined that massive iron-bound oak, then turned to the door on the right side. This he swung open, and vanished into the cavern depths beyond.

The three soldiers glowered, muttered together, watched Grimm with hot angry eyes. One of them snarled at him.

"Speak up, you French dog! Give us an excuse to slit your damned throat!"

Grimm looked at them in silence; words were still beyond

his power. The torch here was guttering out. One of the men brought a lantern, lit it, and hung it on a hook.

Now the light of Mortlake reappeared. He left the right-hand door wide open behind him as he came, and breathing heavily, emerged from the opening. With a grunt of approval he placed his torch in the sconce, and took down the lantern. He was flushed and sweating from exertion, yet spoke with his eternal calmness.

"Get out horses for us all, and saddle them," he ordered. "I see Master Rudolph tied up yonder. Let him loose; tell him to get everybody out of the inn, and to go himself to the castle. You three, await orders from me."

He gave Luther Grimm one steady look, then turned and strode into the passage again. Near the open right-hand door, he hung his lantern on a hook, and himself passed on into the darkness out of sight.

THE AUTHORITY of Mortlake was evidently established and unquestioned. The three men started away and disappeared from Grimm's range of vision. After a time the bellowing voice of Master Rudolph briefly lifted, indicating that the gag, at least, was removed.

Mortlake came into sight again. Now he held in his arms a small keg, from which he let fall a black trail along the passage floor, on past the lantern to the doorway, where he set down the trail. He carried out a double handful of the black contents to where the torch burned, and trailed it along the floor, evidently to test. Grimm realized with sudden frantic wakening that it was powder.

Mortlake reached up for the torch and held it to his test train. The black grains spluttered and gushed up in smoke; the fire ate along the trail, instead of flaring up. The acrid odor, the smoke, died out, and Mortlake put the torch back in its socket.

"Aye," he said, with a satisfied nod. "It's a bit damp. So much the better."

RETURNING TO the keg, he laid a heavy trail of the powder out from the entrance of the cavern; the keg empty, he put it aside, took out his knife, and approached Luther Grimm. That glittering eye of his bored into Grimm.

"You've lived long enough, and you'll not die too quick either," he said, and the intensity of his hatred brought a little quiver into his voice.

"You and your men to hell together, you dog," he went on, with a deliberate cold fury. "I'd like to sink this knife into you, but that's too quick an end to suit me. You can hang there and think about it. I'll put the knife into you, aye, and I'll do it here and now—but not to kill you, understand? You'll hang there and bleed, and when I leave you'll watch the fire take the powder. A whole room full of powder in there, understand? And this time I make sure of you—"

He turned his head, listening. Muffled hammering sounds came from that left-hand door at the end of the passage, where Cavaignac was trying vainly to get out. Mortlake snarled mirthlessly.

"Pound away! Hear them, Grimm? Those doors are built to withstand anything. They'll hold. Your run of luck is through. Now to prick you, so you'll die slow but certain—"

He thumbed the knife-point and stepped forward, his face aflame suddenly with venom and hatred. Suddenly he checked himself and glanced around. Master Rudolph was coming, and behind him the three soldiers who had set him free. His voice burst out with a bellow of fury, that fetched the astonished Mortlake quickly around.

"Mortlake! You damned Englishman, you liar!" cried the innkeeper. "You lied to us! Why didn't you tell us Count Otto was poisoned, was dead? You and she both lied to us!"

Mortlake growled like a dog disturbed at meat.

"Off about your business—clear out!" he snapped viciously. "I had nothing to do with it. She did it. She told me later. If he's dead—"

"So it's true!" An overwhelming rage caught up Master Rudolph, and he shook in the grip of it. As he glared, he caught sight of the keg and the powder train.

"What's that—*Herr Gott!*" he roared furiously. "Why, you accursed English whelp, you're laying a powder train—"

Without warning, he flung himself forward in blind fury.

Mortlake shouted at him, screamed at him, plunged with the knife; but the huge Rudolph had him, seized him in those enormous hands, lifted, shook him like a rat. The knife flashed, dripped red, flashed again—then Mortlake was hurled bodily against the wall with a crash that fairly shook the old structure.

But Master Rudolph, blood pouring from his body, choked and fell, lifeless.

One instant of wild terrorized silence; then the three staring soldiers found voice, erupted in oaths and wild cries.

"Out of here!" yelled one of them frantically. "Get out—to the castle, to the castle!"

They turned and ran for it. Luther Grimm shouted after them, but in vain. Frantic flight and nothing else held them frenzied. They ran to the horses Cavaignac had left standing, mounted, and went clattering madly out of the courtyard.

Now everything fell silent again, except for the dim muffled sounds from inside the caverns where Cavaignac was blocked. Grimm twisted at the cords holding his wrists, writhed, put his weight on them until blood flecked his torn skin; but they held strong and fast.

Grimm shouted again, hoping to reach some of the women locked in the inn.

MORTLAKE, STILL gripping his bloody knife, was roused by that voice. He moved, he came to one elbow. His head dragged up, and his one eye fastened on Grimm with a baleful glare. He had been badly hurt by that terrific crash. He tried to gain his feet, but could not rise; a trickle of blood came from one corner of his mouth as he gasped.

He dragged himself forward, his dilated eye unwavering on the figure of Grimm. Inch by inch, foot by foot, he drew himself on. He was so close that Grimm could see how his facial muscles quivered to every effort. Slowly he came to one knee, hand gripping knife. A supreme exertion shook him as he poised there—and suddenly Grimm's foot shot out.

The kick caught Mortlake under the chin. It lifted him backward and sent him sliding. His arms were outflung; he lay quiet, senseless.

Grimm tore at his bonds again, only to relax and groan with the hurt of his bleeding wrists. Abruptly, his head lifted. A new sound reached him.

Horses clattering, wheels rolling and squeaking—a carriage coming into the courtyard, where the torches were now at their last gasp. He could not see from where he stood, but he could hear his name being called—the voice of Marie!

Hoarsely, he found tongue.

OLD JACQUES was the first to reach the spot, guided by Grimm's voice. He caught up the knife of Mortlake and cut Grimm free; as he sheared away the bloodstained cords, Marie appeared.

"Oh, comrade—I should have gone with you!" She caught hold of Grimm, clung to him, held him off and looked at him. "You're hurt, hurt—"

"I'm not hurt; all's well now. You're just in time—you don't know how just in time!" Grimm laughed shakily. "Here, wait."

He caught the lantern from its hook. One glance at the prostrate Mortlake showed there was nothing to fear from him now. Grimm ran into the cavern passage and came to the doors at the end. Next moment he had heaved away the massive bar, and the left-hand door swung open.

Cavaignac and his men poured forth, hoarse, wearied, stammering with chagrin. Grimm led them outside, took Marie's arm, and urged her away from that shambles into the courtyard. He halted, deaf to the excited questions of the girl.

"Do as I say and talk later; we must act, before Osbrock's men get here from the castle. Back into your carriage! Jacques, drive out of the courtyard, around to the side, and wait there in the road. I'll come soon. Don't talk—do it!"

His driving force compelled them; Jacques scrambled for the carriage seat, Marie followed. Grimm turned to Cavaignac. He and his men had seen the body of their comrade, slain by Mortlake's knife, and were cursing hotly.

"One of you, go turn those women out of the place. Take a torch with you and set it to the curtains, the walls, anything! Fire the place. The other three, clear out all the horses here except fresh animals for us; get these saddled and waiting. Drive all the rest out of the courtyard. Cavaignac! Come along."

The men scattered hastily. The carriage was moving. Grimm faced back toward that cavern entrance. The torch there was burning low in its socket, but would last for a time.

"It was hell in there." Cavaignac was speaking. "We found the other entrance; it curves around and comes out farther down the stables, but it was barred. Those doors must be a foot thick; our pistol balls had no effect on the locks. The smoke damned near choked us. We found two bodies, chained in rooms—one man, one woman. Both dead, and not long dead either—"

"They'll be soon buried," said Grimm curtly.

"Monsieur!" a shout came from the man who had gone to free the women. "They broke out a window and are gone, all of them! Shall I fire the place?"

"Do it quickly," rejoined Grimm.

What to do with Mortlake, lying there helpless? He frowned, undecided, as he led Cavaignac toward the stables. Abruptly, he came to a halt; there was a scrape of feet from the darkness, then the blast of a pistol. Cavaignac staggered back. Another pistol jetted red; Grimm felt the hot wind of the ball on his cheek.

"Damn you!" It was Mortlake, cursing like a fiend. "You damned American, I'll see you hanged yet for the rebel you are—by heaven, I'll have you and that woman halted and thrown into—"

His voice died out, with another scuff of feet. Grimm darted forward and his lantern sent a feeble light into the passage. He saw the figure of Mortlake just vanishing from sight through the door by which Cavaignac had formerly passed.

GRIMM HALTED. Behind him was coming Cavaignac, one hand pressed against a bleeding shoulder.

"Well, captain, you've got him!" Cavaignac laughed. "As I know to my cost, he can't get out of that hell-hole."

Grimm put down his lantern. He went to the left-hand door and leaned his weight against it. Slowly it moved, and clanged shut. Picking up the heavy bar, Grimm set it in the sockets. He turned to Cavaignac.

"You're hurt?"

"I can ride."

"Come on out of here."

They passed out again, by the bodies of Rudolph and the others, to the courtyard. Hooves clattered; the new-saddled horses were ready, the others were being driven out. The man sent to fire the inn came running.

"It's done," he panted. "Fired in two places."

"Help Cavaignac," said Grimm. "Leave one horse for me. Mount and ride; join the carriage, ride on a hundred yards, and wait for me."

"But, monsieur—"

"Do as you're told."

Cavaignac was assisted into a saddle. The others rode away with him. One horse remained, saddled and waiting. Grimm took the reins and led the horse behind him, back to where the torch smoked in its sconce.

ALL WERE gone. The courtyard was silent; but from the Inn of the Last Virgin lifted a red glow, a subdued crackle of flames taking hold. Grimm, with a thin smile, looked into the passage opening.

"Aye. He's in his own trap; let him take the consequences."

He reached up to the stub of the torch and took it down. The horse plunged, startled by the flame so close; stooping, Grimm thrust the torch into the powder-trail at his feet. The damp powder was slow to catch. Suddenly it flared up, and fire began to run along the black trail.

With one leap, Grimm was in the saddle, turning the horse, riding hard. He came out across the courtyard, passed the gates, swung into the road. From the inn, as he passed outside, came a roaring crescendo of crackling flame. Ahead showed the carriage and horses.

"Go!" shouted Grimm. "Quickly!"

Carriage and horses moved and gathered speed. Grimm caught up with them, and then slowed pace beside the carriage. Sudden fear caught at him; time interminable had passed, nothing had happened. Perhaps the damp powder had failed.

"Where to, now?" demanded Jacques. "Where to, monsieur?"

Almost with the words, the earth shook and thundered. From the inn behind, a spout of flame leaped skyward. From Luther Grimm broke a harsh laugh. Marie was reaching up from the carriage; he leaned over in the saddle and caught her hand, and laughed again, but not harshly this time.

"Where to?" repeated Luther Grimm. "To America—eh, Marie?"

The pressure of her fingers replied.

ABOUT THE AUTHOR

H. BEDFORD-JONES is a Canadian by birth, but not by profession, having removed to the United States at the age of one year. For over twenty years he has been more or less profitably engaged in writing and traveling. As he has seldom resided in one place longer than a year or so and is a person of retiring habits, he is somewhat a man of mystery; more than once he has suffered from unscrupulous gentlemen who impersonated him—one of whom murdered a wife and was subsequently shot by the police, luckily after losing his alias.

The real Bedford-Jones is an elderly man, whose gray hair and precise attire give him rather the appearance of a retired foreign diplomat. His hobby is stamp collecting, and his collection of Japan is said to be one of the finest in existence. At present writing he is en route to Morocco, and when this appears in print he will probably be somewhere on the Mojave Desert in company with Erle Stanley Gardner.

Questioned as to the main facts in his life, he declared there was only one main fact, but it was not for publication; that his life had been uneventful except for numerous financial losses, and that his only adventures lay in evading adventurers. In his younger years he was something of an athlete, but the encroachments of age preclude any active pursuits except that of motoring. He is usually to be found poring over his stamps, working at his typewriter, or laboring in his California rose garden, which is one of the sights of Cathedral Cañon, near Palm Springs.

www.ingramcontent.com/pod-product-compliance
Lightning Source LLC
Chambersburg PA
CBHW061523020726
47502CB00006B/2208